"I promised Rusty I'd find Dale a date to the engineering awards night next Friday," Casey explained.

"Um, obvious? You're single. Dale's single. Right?" Ashleigh widened her eyes at Casey.

"No way!"

"You promised—you deliver." Ashleigh folded her pink ZBZ T-shirt *very* definitively. "And hello? The all-Greek formal is next *Saturday* night, and I see a roommate and former president who is, dare I say, dateless?"

That was the last thing Casey needed to be reminded of. "Maybe I can take Dale," she joked.

"See! That's the attitude of a ZBZ."

"Ash! Kidding!"

"So you have two problems. One is finding someone to go with Dale next Friday, and we solved that. You're going with Dale."

Casey tested the sentence. "I'm going with Dale."

"See? Not so bad. Second problem—we have to find a superhot guy who you have not previously dated and therefore have no emotional hang-ups over—"

"I am not hung up on Cappie—"

"—to be your date to the formal. We have a whole week! Seven great days to find a great guy. How hard can it be?"

Don't miss *Greek: Best Frenemies*
coming in October 2010

And watch for more great Greek titles!

GRΣΣK

double date

marsha warner

HARLEQUIN®
TEEN

HARLEQUIN®
TEEN

Recycling programs for this product may not exist in your area.

ISBN-13: 978-0-373-21014-5

GREEK: DOUBLE DATE

This edition published by arrangement with Harlequin Books S.A.

For questions and comments about the quality of this book please contact us at Customer_eCare@Harlequin.ca.

www.HarlequinTEEN.com

Printed in U.S.A.

For my brother Jason

chapter one

If Casey Cartwright was sure of anything, it was that if she had to spend her last hours anywhere, the Zeta Beta Zeta house was not the worst place to do it. The sorority house with its dignified white colonial exterior had been her home for the best years of her life, and surely her sisters would give her a decent burial, despite the undignified nature of her final hours perched atop the center island of the house kitchen.

The second thing that she was sure of she decided to voice, if only to pass the time. "If this is how we go, at least we're doing it together."

"Speak for yourself," Ashleigh said, leaning over the edge with a ladle in hand. "I'm not starving to death when there are Cheeseritos five feet away." Unfortunately for Ashleigh Howard, ZBZ president and Casey's heroine, not even a positive attitude could make the ladle she was holding longer, and it dropped with a crash to the ground. "Crap!" A gap still stood between them and the cheesy nourishment on the far counter. "Fisher!"

Ashleigh's boyfriend, the ZBZ house hasher, stood in the doorway, motorcycle helmet under one arm. "Why are you squatting on the counter like stranded—"

"Mouse!"

"Mouse!"

The aforementioned menace made his latest squeak, darting in and out of view between the cabinets. At which point Fisher, their manly savior, dropped his helmet not in a desperate bid to rescue them from the invading rodent but to leap up—albeit in a manly way—onto the counter, landing between them.

They stared. He squirmed. "Sorry. My freshman dorm was infested. I still have nightmares."

Casey and Ashleigh sighed.

"Do you know how long we've been up here? I am this close to eating the box of salad croutons."

"And I am this close to sharing them," Casey said. "Rebecca, don't!"

Rebecca Logan was not easily startled, not even when she was in her pink pajamas and matching robe, giving a softer edge to her often-icy exterior. The daughter of former-Senator Logan—now divorced and beset by a scandal involving a prostitution ring—had been through a lot and was not easily perturbed. Not that she had been easily startled while her father was still a distinguished senator. She'd always had a politician's craftiness. Rebecca's often-nefarious expression, complemented by her brown eyes and dark hair, made her a frightening figure when she wanted to be. Fortunately, that was not all the time, and she was by no means dour. While her tone was always serious, she could and would make jokes—sometimes at other people's expense—and she got along with her sorority sisters…most of the time. "What?"

"Mouse!" they shouted, all three in unison.

Rebecca did not jump, or shriek, or have any other reaction comparable to theirs. She looked down at the floor, then at them, then moved past them all to the refrigerator in the back. "People keep them as pets. Once you've seen one fed to a boa constrictor, you've seen them all." She pulled down a plastic bowl from above the fridge and unceremoniously dropped it on the floor, trapping the intruder without so much as a blink. "To the victor goes the spoils." With that, she grabbed the entire bag of Cheeseritos and left.

"So—not our most glorious moment," Casey said as she slid off the counter, only to discover her feet had fallen asleep. "Ow." Casey took almost everything in stride—or at least appeared to, with her natural confidence and dignified presentation. Her long blond hair was—usually—perfectly settled on her shoulders, and her mischievous smile and blue eyes disarmed most ill-intentioned people—except for rival sorority sisters, who seemed to have some kind of immunity.

"Yeah, best we never speak of this again," Ashleigh said. Ashleigh was an ideal sorority sister in all the good ways—she was friendly, at times selfless, and eager to please while maintaining her self-respect. She was thin, her wild outfits complementing her mocha-colored skin and perfectly combed black hair. She was fashionable without being a diva, and graceful without being a ballet dancer. Ashleigh gave Fisher a kiss and her sweetest smile. "And, Fisher, can you empty that bowl?" She pointed to the captured mouse without looking directly at it. "You know, kitchen duties. Because it's in the kitchen." She offered no consolation at the sight of his horrified expression.

Casey decided it was best to leave presidential matters—such as designating duties within the house—to her president and friend. Casey's brief tenure as interim president had given her a new appreciation for the job. The previous year, a pledge named Jen K—admitted because she was a legacy—had written an exposé on Greek life, specifically within the sacred confines of the ZBZ house, which earned Jen her first Associated Press credit, and put ZBZ on probation by ZBZ Nationals. Frannie, the sitting president, had ordered the girls to lie to the National ZBZ officer who'd come to assess the situation, but Casey stood up for the truth—and herself—and was named president instead. When she'd finally run for the position officially, it was against Frannie, who had failed to graduate and was spending a fifth year at Cyprus-Rhodes. Because of their negative campaigns, they'd both lost to Ashleigh, who wasn't even running. The entire episode had given Casey a taste for politics but a sense of cynicism when it came to Greek life; only Ashleigh and her responsibility to her sisters had brought Casey back to the house for her senior year of college.

Putting those thoughts behind her, Casey would have finally returned to her and Ashleigh's room for the evening and recovered from her temporary captivity in the kitchen if not for the sudden appearance of her brother in the hallway. "Rusty! What are you doing here? You know boys aren't allowed in the bedrooms of the house, especially after hours. Do you know what time it is?"

"You sound like Mom."

It was accurate, but she wasn't obligated to acknowledge that. "What are you doing here?"

"I was here at a reasonable hour," Rusty insisted, "but they said you'd be right out, like, two hours ago. And then one hour ago. And then—"

Rather than explain to him that she'd spent the past two hours huddling in fear after an ice-cream run went awry thanks to a mouse, she interrupted him. "What is it?"

Rusty took a deep breath, as he often did rather dramatically before releasing whatever had been bottled up in his thin, geeky frame for so long. Looking at Rusty, one would not assume he was the type to mix with fraternity guys. He was thin, almost bony, and his hair was brown—rust-colored, in fact, appropriate given his nickname. He spoke quickly, often nervously, as if knowing he would spit out something ridiculous before he even said anything, but he made up for it by being a wonderful hopeless romantic. "The honors engineering program is having an awards dinner on Friday, and I need a date."

With all the skill of a ZBZ big sister, Casey briefly thought through her interactions with Jordan, Rusty's girlfriend, since she had last seen her with Rusty. Jordan hadn't *seemed* in emotional turmoil from a breakup. "Jordan can't go?"

"It's not for *me,*" Rusty said sheepishly. "Dale needs a date." Assigned as his freshman roommate, Dale Kettlewell had not seemed like a good prospect for lasting friendship for Rusty, as Dale was a Bible-Belt, Greek-hating, fundamentalist Baptist who constantly preached chastity and virtue. He even played in a band called Darwin Lied. Time, and Dale's nearly selfless commitment to friendship, had proved Casey's initial assumptions upon seeing Dale's Confederate flag hanging on the dorm wall wrong. For their sophomore year, Dale and Rusty were sharing an apartment off campus. "He's being honored for having a 4.0 grade point average, and he's self-conscious about it. And his purity pledge brothers aren't exactly helping him out. They're going to Fire Island that weekend, *again*."

"Fire Island?"

"I know, I looked it up on Google." Dale's ignorance on certain issues was not something Rusty always wanted to defeat. "Don't tell Dale. He'll either go on a holy crusade when they get back or into another depression of biblical proportions. His only other friend besides me is Calvin, and before you say it, he can't take Calvin."

"I wasn't going to say it." Casey imagined Calvin's reaction to being romantically linked with Dale. "Definitely not going to say it. So why are you asking me?"

"Because the ZBZ Sisterhood is comprised of the best and the brightest of our generation, pillars of both the female and larger community, venerable diamonds in the rough, who are meant to be a beacon of light, drawing all in and discriminating against no one. Even lonely sophomores with a 4.0 grade point average and a purity ring."

Casey studied him. "Have you been reading the ZBZ pledge manual?"

Rusty shrugged. "I had to do something for two hours. You shouldn't leave it around if you don't want people to read it. Please, you have to help Dale out. He's desperate."

"I thought he was dating your landlady."

"They broke up. Specifically, she dumped him. Normally I would be happy about that, but he's totally depressed. He's so desperate he doesn't even *know* how desperate he is," Rusty said. "She had this, like, cougar spell on him. He thought he was in love."

"And you want me to ask a ZBZ to go? Out of what, pity?"

"At this point, I don't care what it is." Rusty sighed. "Please. I need someone to be the Sister of Mercy, extolling the highest virtues of sisterhood and good nature toward her fellow man while shining a beacon of light into the darkness that is—"

Casey put up her hand. "Okay, you can stop quoting the handbook *right now.* Please. Just…what about Jordan?"

"Uh, she's going with me?"

"Right." She couldn't believe she hadn't thought of that, and chalked it up to rodent-related exhaustion. "Fine. I'll ask the sisters—but it's hands-off for the evening."

"It's *Dale.* Just feed whoever it is some lines about the importance of feminine virtue, and he'll leave enough room between them for a holy spirit to fit into. Actually, that's a good one. The holy spirit one. She should try that."

"Do Baptists believe in a holy spirit?"

"He tells me to flood my body with it."

"Okay, Rus. That's creepy."

"Yeah, but I definitely prefer it to walking in on a Dale and Sheila make-out session." He shuddered. "Thank you for this."

"I'm only asking them. I can't make them say yes."

"You're the ZBZ pledge educator. You can make pledges say yes."

"Not if I want them to stay pledges. Now go, before people start thinking ZBZ is a dating service." She pushed her brother out the door—never a hard thing to do, considering his size—and headed up for the night, ignoring one last manly yell from the kitchen.

"So? Did it work?"

Rusty was barely in the door and his girlfriend, Jordan, was on him—not literally, unfortunately, but with questions, shouted from the couch of his apartment.

One year ago, Rusty Cartwright would have been able to

boast little to no persuasive powers over his sister. He'd entered Cyprus-Rhodes as an honors engineering student with hardly any social life and a big sister who had apparently informed no one that her little brother existed. They were classic opposites, socially, until Rusty decided to pledge the notorious party-hard fraternity, Kappa Tau Gamma. Being an honors engineering student and a fraternity pledge was sometimes difficult to balance, but it gave him a newfound willpower—and, it seemed, a backbone when it came to wooing women. Granted, that backbone was usually provided by some helpful words from his fraternity big brother and Kappa Tau president, Cappie, but it was there all the same, and had won him a girlfriend who also happened to be, conveniently, a ZBZ pledge.

"Thanks for the pledge book," he said, sitting down next to her. "That totally sealed the deal."

"So who's he going with?"

"I don't know yet. Casey said she would talk to the pledges." He added, "Not you, obviously, because you *have* a date."

"And a date to the All-Greek Formal."

"And a date to the All-Greek Formal," he repeated, trying not to sound too excited about it. *All-Greek* meant, of course, that all the formality should make it as uninteresting as possible, and as a Kappa Tau he would have no business going if he wasn't loyally dating a ZBZ. But Rusty, ever the romantic, truly couldn't wait to escort Jordan to the event. She was not his first girlfriend, but she was his best girlfriend, in his humble opinion. She was intelligent, she could be geeky and she loved him. It also helped that she was beautiful—long blond hair and a warm smile, and yet an offbeat tomboyish sense of style that went well with the Kappa Taus, even if it made her somewhat unusual at ZBZ. "I'll be there for emotional support. In a tux."

"Tuxes are sexy." Jordan kissed him. "They make everyone look like James Bond."

The silence that followed was not long-lasting, as Dale appeared in the doorway, a wool robe over his clothing. "Hey. Make room for the holy spirit. At least on the knitting couch."

"Nailed it," Rusty whispered, and he and Jordan laughed together.

"Nikki. Tiffany. Christy. Why am I striking out?"

"Because people with *I* sounds at the end of their name are jinxed?" Ashleigh said from her end of their room, where she was sorting laundry. "Seriously, you have to let up. Remember what happened when you talked me into being Rusty's date to our formal last year?"

Casey grimaced. That had gotten a little awkward when Ash had wound up having a decent time only to have Rusty misunderstand and make a move on her. Luckily they'd straightened things out and ended that evening on a positive note.

She certainly wasn't getting anywhere now by going full steam ahead. Even though the All-Greek Formal wasn't until the night after the honors engineering awards, the pledges all seemed to have dates—or other suitable excuses—for not being available for a pity escort, and they were ready to offer them up before she even said what the date was or whom they would be going with. "You know one pledge even used the hair-washing excuse? As if that works on other girls."

"You can't order anyone on a date."

"It would be in the spirit of sisterhood."

"Face it, Casey—if escorting engineering students without social lives was a pledge tradition, this house would be deader than IKI during a fat-camp excursion week," Ashleigh said, making Casey smile, at least at the mention of the now-former sorority Iota Kappa Iota. "If honors engineers wanted to date sorority girls, they would join fraternities, like normal guys. Isn't that what Psi Phi Pi is for? The *Revenge of the Nerds* fraternity?"

"Not all guys are meant to be fraternity guys." She paused. "Max wasn't."

Ashleigh sighed. "I wasn't going to say his name, but now that you brought it up, yeah. And didn't he totally have trouble asking you out? Didn't you practically have to ask *him* out after using your brother as an undercover agent to find out if he liked you?"

"Yes." It wasn't worth denying anything about the intricacies of formerly dating Max, engineering grad student and nonfraternity guy, to Ashleigh, who knew every detail. It had been at its best, magical, and at its worst, exhausting. But there had been more good times than bad before they broke up and Max left for England. "The point is, I promised Rusty."

"He can't ask you for the impossible. You can't betray your sisterhood."

"I'm *his* sister. That's why I said yes!"

"I mean your *other* sisterhood. *Duh*."

Ashleigh had a point and denying it would only drag out the conversation. "I still need to find a date for Dale."

"Um, obvious? You're single, Dale's…single, right?"

"He's getting over being dumped by his cougar landlady. Sheila."

"Ew, TMI."

"You asked."

A precisely folded blue tank top landed on Ashleigh's dark

comforter. Ashleigh was an expert at folding laundry on her pristine white bedspread. "So, Dale is truly pathetic to the point where he doesn't see his own pathetic-ness, and you don't have the excuse of being attached. You promised Rusty a ZBZ sister. Go with Dale."

"No! Ew!"

"That's your reaction but you would ask a pledge to go with him?"

"It's not that." Casey struggled for an answer. "I think Dale has a crush on me. Every time we see each other he's like… worse than he normally is. And once, I caught him trying to slip a demo CD for his band in my sorority mailbox."

Her ZBZ sister and president was ever the pragmatist. "It's not mix-tape bad."

"It's not mix-tape bad, but it's bad."

"Then you're obligated to do your part as a ZBZ sister and not force him on a pledge. You promised, you deliver." Ashleigh folded her pink ZBZ T-shirt *very* definitively. "And hello? The All-Greek Formal is next Saturday night and I see a roommate and former president who is, dare I say, dateless?"

That was the last thing she needed to be reminded of. "Maybe I can take Dale."

"See! That's the attitude of a ZBZ."

"Ash! Kidding!"

"Well you broke up with Max and you won't ask Cappie. So who does that leave?"

"At least I'm not taking the house hasher," Casey said with a wink.

"Fisher is a university student with a diversified portfolio of extracurricular activities. And a hunk. And, yes, he cleans our kitchens. I can't discriminate. We're supposed to extol the highest emanations of virtue, a beacon of light shining upon our fellow—"

"Okay, why is everyone quoting the ZBZ pledge book today?"

"Is that what it's from? I heard it somewhere and thought it sounded good." She eased herself onto Casey's bed. Ashleigh, Casey's trusted best friend since their pledge days, was the only one allowed to sit down on Casey's bed, and she did so with the authority of a saintly wise man ascending from the heavens, albeit with curlers and perfect nail polish. "So you have two problems. One is finding someone to go with Dale, and we solved that. You're going with Dale."

Casey tested the sentence. "I'm going with Dale."

"See? Not so bad. Second problem—we have to find a superhot guy who you have not previously dated and therefore have no emotional hang-ups over—"

"I am not hung up on Cappie—"

"—to be your date to the formal. We have practically a whole week! Six great days to find a great guy. How hard can it be?"

chapter two

"...and that is why no Kappa Tau brother will be patronizing the fine establishment known as the Gentleman's Choice on Tuesdays or any other night where the lovely lady known as Dusty is performing. Pledges, you're on your own." Cappie banged his presidential gavel against the wooden chair's armrest. "Any questions?"

Looking around, one might have suspected it was too early in the morning for such a serious conversation at Kappa Tau's fraternity house, but it was actually two in the afternoon. Members had woken from sleep long enough to eat cereal and congregate in the somewhat musty living room for their weekly meeting. Empty cups from last night's party were strewn about and there was a new stain on the old sofa, adding to the massive collection of old stains from years past.

Beaver raised his hand. "What if she changes nights? Or there's another stripper there we want to see?"

As usual, Cappie had an immediate answer. "Beaver, while we here at Kappa Tau do not discourage the profession of stripping, there are times when we must band together in a crusade against those who lower themselves to do something as terrible as debase a brother by severely overcharging for services and then not accepting Wade's mom's credit card, lest they encourage other strippers to think we here are made of cash." Cappie was tall, broad and fit, but otherwise nothing like the jocks of other fraternities. His brown hair was wavy and perpetually tousled, his clothing looked a step away from qualifying for a laundry pile, and he was a notorious flirt, able to charm women after one look into his piercing blue eyes. Cappie's oratory abilities—and occasional sense of responsibility, at least when it came to protecting and maintaining Kappa Tau—had earned him the position of president in his junior year, a position he'd reclaimed by "calling it" fast enough when they forgot to hold elections. Now a senior, he was facing his final year at Cyprus-Rhodes and wanted to go out with a bang. He did not want to repeat his fraternity big brother Egyptian Joe's eight-year college experience. He wanted to have fun, then graduate. Possibly.

"In other words, stay away from Dusty," Wade said. "And don't ask if she accepts quarters."

"We are not holding it against the club itself," Cappie said. "We will continue to actively patronize them when said lap dancer is not present, and at no other times. Is that clear?" He looked up as light shone in the faces of some hungover members when Rusty opened the front door and entered the living room. "Spitter, is that clear?"

Rusty could tell right away that the correct answer was, "Yes, Cappie."

"Good." There was no need to bother Rusty with the particulars in front of everyone and further slow down the meeting.

Recounting the Dusty incident for information purposes was degrading enough. Cappie continued, "Next issue… Pickle? Arm?"

Pickle raised his arm, and Cappie made a quick inspection of the notes written in marker on it.

"Okay, the All-Greek Formal is…next Saturday? Pickle, what did I say about your handwriting?" Since Pickle was not in a condition to answer, he went on, "As with all Panhellenic-IFC formals, the attendance of at least one member of each house is required."

Everyone started speaking at once.

"Not it."

"Can I take my girlfriend?"

"She's not your girlfriend. You just think that stripper likes you."

"Make the pledges go," Arrowhead mumbled, chewing on a stick of beef jerky.

"It has to be an active," Wade said. "I have a girlfriend, but she's out of town. And I'll miss the party."

"I'm going," Rusty said.

"See? Spitter shows all the enthusiasm of a true Kappa Tau," Cappie said, "to step in and sacrifice himself to the university gods so that his fair brothers can get drunk and party with women not constricted by formal attire, low-cut though it may be."

"Dude, did you just call us 'fair'?"

"Yes, Beaver, and you will not interrupt my dramatic flourishes," Cappie said. "Spitter, you have our thanks."

"I was going to say, I'm going as Jordan's date, and Jordan said that presidential attendance is required."

"Ah, yes, so good of you to be observant," Cappie said sarcastically. "Actually the rules for the All-Greek Formal stipulate that *a* president is required to attend, unless some medical or family emergency prevents him or her from doing so. Hence the title of the party we'll be throwing that night, 'Operation Operation.'"

"I thought that was just to get women to show up in nurses' uniforms."

"That's what we tell pledges," Cappie said. "Welcome to being an active. Now—anything else?" Several groans told him the meeting was not going to continue much longer without the actives finding sustenance and/or a miracle hangover cure. He banged his gavel again. "Meeting adjourned."

As KTs dispersed to other places on the couch or to the kitchen, Rusty approached Cappie. He didn't have to explain why he was late—he had a science lab that ran into meetings this semester, and even Cappie's attempted seduction of the scheduling assistant hadn't changed that. "Why don't you just go to the formal? I know you have the clothing, and the drinks are free. And it'll make Kappa Tau look good."

"Spitter, when do I ever take a chance to make the house look good?"

After a calculated moment, Rusty said, "Never."

"With one minor exception. Of course I'm going. But I would prefer to leave early and return to the house to be greeted by concerned girls in nurse costumes. And if anything were to happen on campus that was in any way suspicious, for once, I would have a perfect alibi."

In the ZBZ house living room, a similar conversation was occurring, though far less confidently.

"Maybe Rusty could find you a date," Jordan said to her big

sister and official sponsor within the pledge system, Casey. "He does owe you one."

"Please, my little brother find *me* a date to a formal?" Casey said. "I think the stars would have to collide in some universe-destroying fashion for that to happen. I'm a ZBZ. I am perfectly capable of finding a date who is cute and nice and not creepy and not someone I've already dated and not a pity date." She waved it off as Jordan left the room, and Ashleigh took a closer seat so that they were less likely to be overheard.

"There's Cappie," Ashleigh said, with a loud whisper. Casey had dated Cappie for most of freshman year, before breaking up with him for neglecting her, not to mention his lack of ambition. She spent the next two years of her life deeply involved with his former roommate, the current Omega Chi president, Evan Chambers. That relationship had also ended in disaster, the breakup perhaps made more painful by age and the seriousness of their involvement, and she had then moved on to an engineering grad student named Max before realizing, ultimately, that she still had feelings for Cappie, and possibly always would, despite never having been able to rely on him. But Ashleigh, her ever-bubbly self, continued, "He has to go anyway. He's KT president."

"The KT house is throwing an operating-room theme party. He'll get out of the formal by faking illness." Or that was what she was hoping. If Cappie did put in an appearance, her own presence would not go unnoticed by him, and she would spend the evening avoiding that look in his eyes that made her stomach flutter. While having an embarrassing run-in with Cappie was par for the social course in Casey-land, she would prefer it not to occur in front of Panhellenic and the Inter-Fraternity Council.

"How about Calvin?"

"Um, yeah, just announce to the world that I couldn't find a date? Besides, isn't Calvin seeing someone?" Bringing an outed gay guy was definitely a pity date, even if he was an Omega Chi and very cool.

"If he is, he totally won't bring him to the formal," Ashleigh said. "But I see your point there. What about Facebook?"

"Again, ew. Anyone at college who needs to go online to get a date couldn't find one face-to-face on campus. Cyprus-Rhodes is not that big."

"Twitter? Or is that even worse? I don't really know what Twitter is. I just like the word."

"It is a fun word. But it's worse. I think." Her contact with computer social networks was limited anyway. She still relied on the tried-and-true cell phone texting to her sisters as communication. "Okay, I'm sure it's worse."

"Well, you just have to face facts. A hot guy is not just going to walk in here and offer to take you." Ashleigh's eyes darted to the door. "Ooh! Man in the house!" It was the instinctive call to announce when a guy entered, even a known one. Fortunately neither of them were in their pajamas, but some robed sisters scattered as Ashleigh went to greet him. "Can I help you?"

"Uh, hi." He smiled shyly with his adorable baby-blue eyes. "I'm the new assistant to Dean Bowman."

"Oh!" Ashleigh said with semijoyous surprise, not modulating her voice at all. Casey was always amazed at how she did that. "How can I help you?"

"Hi," he repeated when Casey approached, not to her but to Ashleigh, as if he was checking her mental condition for too much enthusiasm. "There are some rules for the All-Greek Formal—standard stuff—but I need the Zeta Beta Zeta president to sign this sheet…" As he produced the folded piece of paper, Ashleigh winked at Casey and snatched it out of his hands.

"Let me get a pen!" she practically squealed, and ran into the kitchen for some reason, leaving the two of them alone in the front hallway.

"Was that President Howard?"

At a loss to explain Ashleigh's behavior, Casey said, "Yes. Oh—and I'm Casey Cartwright, ZBZ sister and pledge educator."

"Robert Howell," he said, and accepted her handshake. "Rob, really. Only my parents call me Robert. And Dean Bowman. And…everyone who doesn't like me, I guess." He frowned, as if trying to think of something. He had a rather attractive square jaw. His official university-style clothing—meaning preppy—suited him, even if he didn't look comfortable in it. And he avoided the bed-head look that was so dated by having his sandy-blond hair cleanly cropped and trimmed. "Weren't you ZBZ president once?"

"Interim president, technically," she said. "Between Frannie and Ashleigh."

"And Frannie Morgan was president of IKI."

"Yes." She resisted the urge to add *unfortunately,* even though it was tempting.

"Sorry, I just have to keep all this stuff straight. Dean Bowman seems very…particular about keeping track of the Greeks. I'm new, and he wrote the recommendation for my transfer, so…"

"Oh, you're a transfer student?"

"From Cornell. I needed a new atmosphere. Anyway, yeah, I just started as a junior here. Still getting used to the warm weather." He squirmed in his wool suit jacket with the university lapels. "I'm work-study, so the job with Dean Bowman is good. No heavy lifting." He laughed, and she laughed with him.

"At least you're not a sorority hasher—though it does pay well."

"A hasher—that's someone who does the kitchen work and cleaning?" At her nod he shrugged again. "I'm not that familiar with sororities. This is the first house I've actually been inside."

"Well, I'm glad ZBZ was your first," she said as Ashleigh returned.

"Okay. Form-ege," Ashleigh said, returning the signed form.

"You get to keep the yellow copy," Rob said, and tore it off for her. "Thanks."

"Thank *you,*" Ashleigh said, a little overenthusiastically, and he left. She immediately turned to Casey and said, *"So?"*

"So what?"

"So cute guy enters right when you need him, and I give you time for small talk. What's he like?"

"Ashleigh, I had all of two minutes with him. His name is Rob and he's a transfer. That's all I know. I wasn't grilling him for information." She added, "But he was cute."

"Oh, my God, cute and *hot.* That chiseled jaw… I'm tempted to take him for myself if we need a new hasher."

"Ash! Fisher!"

"I know, I know."

"Besides, this is not some succubi house where we consume all men who enter. Even if he kind of looked like he thought it was. Nervous guys can be so adorable."

"Suck-you-what?"

"A succubus is a demon from medieval folklore who would take the form of a beautiful woman in order to seduce a man and drain his life essence," Casey said before she knew what was coming out of her mouth. "Sorry. Freshman year, Myths and Folklore. I took it as my history requirement."

"Wow, that sounds much more interesting than Greek philosophy."

"You took Greek philosophy?"

She shrugged. "I was a pledge. I thought it would look good. Turns out Plato and Aristotle have nothing to do with ZBZ. Who knew?"

Casey rolled her eyes, but withheld comment.

"So? Did you ask him out?"

"Ash, *two minutes.* I don't know anything about him."

"And you have five days to find out enough to ask him out. Or make him like you so much that he asks you out. How hard can it be?"

"Please. He works for Dean Bowman. Who needs more exposure to Dean Bowman?"

The Amphora Secret Society's meeting hall was at once foreboding and disgusting. Being buried in a room in the foundations of the university between two sewage systems and not marked on any map did that. Though the smell didn't permeate the thick walls, the gloom that brought severity to the proceedings of the ancient society was mainly a result of candlelight on dank surroundings. Still, Evan Chambers would admit, it was atmospheric.

Evan was a typical fraternity guy in many ways, with old-fashioned clothing—sweaters and ties tucked neatly into khakis—and a family legacy of blue bloods. He had light brown hair, almost a dirty blond, and matching blue eyes to accentuate his long face.

He looked up blearily as his old enemy/friend Cappie sat down next to him. They were both berobed and ready for the next round of confessions. The initial purge was done, but members were required to make updates as new events occurred, so they could "continue on the journey to wisdom and knowledge together," as Dean Bowman had put it before he stepped down from his position as leader of the supersecret society.

After shepherding them together and into the society's door, Dean Bowman had stepped down to give the next generation their rightful place. Including Cappie, who during his time as Kappa Tau president had been subject to many of the dean's tirades. Cappie saw the dean too much as an oppressive authority figure and too little as a fellow member to be totally at ease in his presence. Some illusions were harder to shatter than others, especially when Amphora members still had to treat the dean normally in public—not that Cappie ever treated any dean, police officer or authority figure normally. His upbringing was far too anticonformist for that.

Hopefully the next confessor to reveal his or her innermost secrets to society members would have fewer dead pets in their history than the girl who'd spoken at an earlier meeting.

Not that Evan was in the mood to care. The Amphora Society members were supposed to be successful, the best and brightest of their generation. Last year at this time, he'd felt that way. He was dating—and considering marrying—Casey Cartwright, the only girl he'd ever met who didn't want him for his legendary Chambers family inheritance, and he was on his way to becoming Omega Chi president. Now he'd been dumped by Casey, had foolishly and painfully dated social climber Frannie to dull the feeling of loneliness then cheated on her rampantly for reasons he didn't really understand, and finally had collapsed under the weight of the ridiculous responsibilities his parents attached to his trust fund by telling them off and basically asking to be disinherited. And now here he was, answering to Cappie, his freshman-year roommate and former rival for Casey's affections. For the sake of the competition between Omega Chi and Kappa Tau, they remained enemies on the surface, but had started to repair their friendship within the confines of the Amphora Society hall.

"Are you drunk?" Cappie asked, looking at him warily.

"Are you asking?" Evan said with a lopsided grin. "You? Cappie? Of Kappa Tau?"

"See, that's why I'm asking. Because if *I* was drunk, it would be no big deal, even though I happen to be observing my sober hour of the day. To cleanse the body. Cleanliness is next to godliness."

"Not down here."

"Yeah. But my point is that you are drunk and I am sober, so either this is part of some weird new ritual that I was supposed to have heard about when I was passed out at the last meeting, or the Four Horsemen of the Apocalypse approacheth." Cappie eyed Evan as if waiting for an explanation. Knowing Cappie, he wouldn't give up until he either got one or tricked one out of him.

Evan tried to switch topics. "I need to get out of the All-Greek Formal."

"You can't drink yourself into illness, dude. I've tried. Go lick some doorknobs. Or the floor in here." Cappie looked around. "It's not like you don't own a tux. Or is the mighty Evan Chambers afraid of going stag? Because I will not gay-escort you. I still have to pretend to hate you in public."

"Frannie and I broke up."

"Ouch! Rejection." He patted Evan on the shoulder. "It happens to the best of us. And the worst of us. In my vast experience, I can attest that even strippers will reject you."

Evan chuckled. "Really?"

"Did you know they don't take American Express? But seriously, Frannie ditched you? Her meal ticket?"

"That was the problem." And just thinking about it gave Evan a headache. He definitely did not want to have the I-gave-up-my-trust-fund conversation with Cappie—not right now, anyway. "And *I* dumped *her.*"

"*What?* Am I getting crazy in my ears? Because that would be reason to celebrate, and this does not look like a celebratory stupor. I can tell the difference in stupors."

"I bet you can," Evan said.

Thankfully, the first confessor of the night took her place at the front next to the newly elected head of the society.

"Before we begin tonight's confessions with Miss Sarah Franklin, does anyone have a pressing matter to bring before the society?"their new fearless leader asked.

Cappie, of all people, sprang up. "I do."

Brett's eye roll could practically be heard. "Yes, Cappie." Which really meant, *No, Cappie, sit back down.*

But Cappie wasn't interested in taking the hint. Instead he actually went to the front and stood before the other members in their carved wooden chairs. "It is my understanding that the bond between Amphora Society members is our most sacred tradition."

"Yes, Mr. Cappie." The president clearly had a *where are you going with this?* expression on his face.

"I say we not besmirch that bond by ignoring the agony of our sacred brother Mr. Chambers, who is right now mourning the death of his own sacred relationship with a beautiful if slightly ethically questionable woman. We should endeavor, as his society siblings, to support him in his time of need."

"Mr. Chambers has not offered the confessional, if that's what you mean." The president glanced at Evan. "Nor does it appear he wants to."

"This is not about the confessional. Evan doesn't want to explain his problems to another person. He wants us to support him. And I think the best way to support him is to join him in a spirit of revelry over his emerging triumphant from a difficult situation—with some sacred amphora jar wine."

The president, who had not had Cappie's vote, sighed. "Nice try." With his more serious voice, he said to the crowd, "Our initiate is correct in that we should support each other in our times of need. We will all drink the amphora wine together—*after* the meeting and confessionals. Please be seated."

Cappie retook his seat. Evan was the only person not enthusiastic about this turn of events. "So now everyone knows."

"Hey—you didn't have to confess it yourself, and I scheduled a party instead."

"You are making me drown in misery."

"No," Cappie said, nudging him. "I just really like that wine."

chapter three

"Yeah? How much? How can that be? Sushi's not even supposed to be cooked. There has to be some kind of discount. Okay. Fine, e-mail me the cost sheet. Thanks. Bye." Rusty Cartwright shut off his phone, closed his apartment door and collapsed on the couch, his feet hanging off the armrest and his head on the seat cushions.

Dale, in the old-fashioned rocking chair that had made its way into their apartment via his mother, an overenthusiastic garage-sale shopper, was knitting, with a heavy science textbook in his lap. He didn't even look up at Rusty's dramatic entrance. "So is there food for next weekend? Because I could always declare it a public fast." Dale was shorter than Rusty and a little stocky. His dark brown hair was longer, straighter, and fell just below his ears. Like an engineering department student stereotype, he had thick glasses shielding his dark eyes and pale face. Dale was unlike most Cyprus-Rhodes students in a number of ways. For one, he was a die-hard Southerner, yet he rarely spoke with an accent.

"I didn't know you could repent while celebrating," Rusty said. "And, yes, there is food. There's even a meal at the hotel for the people arriving the night before. I finally found a place under the budget."

"It was good of you to volunteer," Dale said. "Gets you away from the House of Sin."

"That's a good name for a strip club."

"It was the name of a strip club in my hometown," Dale said. "It had a great sidewalk for picketing. After school on Fridays, we would celebrate our freedom by heading downtown to save some souls from temptation."

"You know, technically, you could say that you spent your Friday nights in high school at a strip club."

Dale said innocently, "And why would I be tempted to say that?"

Rusty sighed. Male posturing wasn't worth explaining to a Christian fundamentalist who was currently knitting while sitting in a rocking chair. "Anyway, I didn't really volunteer. I mean, I did, but it was more because my advisor heavily suggested I do it if I wanted to keep my place in the honors program."

"I thought you said Dr. Hastings hated you."

"He does."

"Oh." Dale at least got that. He wasn't dumb, after all—that was the entire point of the engineering event. "Well, he is your advisor. Besides, if you had a 4.0 grade point average, this wouldn't be an issue."

"Dale, what was our agreement?"

"That if you got me a date I would stop rubbing your GPA in your face?"

"And you will have a date. I promise." He added, "I'm working on it. That, and feeding a bunch of hungry alumni."

Rusty suspected that Dale wasn't truly over Sheila. That, or just the loneliness of single life was making Dale moody. He had quietly complained until Rusty had ended the conversation by offering to get him a date.

"Hey, do you have the guest list? And can I get a peek?"

"Yes, Microsoft will be there," Rusty said, too tired to get up and get the actual list. "And every other major employer of engineers. But they're sending random people. It's not as if celebrities are gonna be there."

"I'd love to be the Bill Gates of electrical engineering. Make millions of dollars, then give it all away to do missionary work and bring some faith to Africa."

"I think Bill Gates is more about bringing food to Africa."

"You can do that part. You know all about ordering food." Fortunately for Dale he meant it as innocently as he meant everything else, which made Rusty less inclined to punch him. He wasn't a violent person, really—neither of them were—but dealing with advisors and then the demands of cranky alumni was starting to wear on the younger Cartwright. Dale's eyebrows rose hopefully. "Do you think they'll let me play at the after-party?"

"Probably not. All I had to say was the band name and it was shot down. Darwin Lied isn't winning you a lot of fans in the science and technology departments."

"Darwin Lied is not about fans. It's about the music. Maybe Silicon Valley hippie liberals aren't ready for the amazing power of the truth. Did you know evolution is still taught in textbooks without warning labels in forty-nine states?"

"*Yes,* Dale."

"The ignorance of some people. It's an uphill battle."

"Then can you not fight it in front of the rest of the honors engineering program?"

“I promise to hold out until the food comes.”

Rusty decided that would have to be good enough.

For once, Casey was early for her Sunday brunch date with her brother, and Rusty was late. Sad, because he had the food—and when he did arrive, it was bagged and obviously bought in a hurry from the campus bakery, located inside the social action center. Inside, the center was actually quite dismal and littered with posters from protests that neither Casey nor Rusty were a part of, but outside was the beautiful campus green and tables and chairs for students to enjoy the sunshine with their overpriced coffee.

“Croissant. Yum.” She didn’t say it sarcastically, but calling it a brunch really implied a lot more than a croissant. She waited for Rusty to unload, because if he didn’t start talking soon, he would definitely explode.

“My advisor is running me ragged,” he said. “Not academically, but over this awards dinner. I had to find a bidder under the university budget for the food, and the hotel we were supposed to send the alumni to was booked, so I had to talk the receptionist into a better deal at another hotel. I have four days before anyone important arrives and I’m having dreams that everyone goes to the wrong hotel and the only food sent is a giant bagel and I have to explain how I ordered a room-size bagel in front of the dean of the department in my underwear.”

“That’s why I suggested that Ashleigh run for social chair and keep the position for as long as possible, back before she was president. Welcome to the world of event planning.”

“Yeah, I am *not* going into hospitality. And speaking of honors engineering, did you find a date for Dale?”

She raised her hand, but it was more of a lowered wave. "Looks like I'm as desperate as he is for a solution to your problem."

"Don't say that. It'll be Dale's dream come true! But don't be surprised if he asks you to come to the after-party. His band is playing."

"Their music was surprisingly good, but I could do without the gospel lyrics."

"Me, too."

"And the name."

"Me and you and everyone who has ever been part of a university science department and will be at this event, so I really need him not to mention it. *Especially* not in front of the biological advancement engineers." He looked at her directly for the first time, something he didn't tend to do when he was ranting. "Thank you for doing this. This means a lot to me, and it'll mean way more to him. And then to me again if you get him to stop talking about Darwin Lied or his breakup with Sheila."

"He still has a major crush on me, doesn't he?"

Rusty shrugged. "He hasn't mentioned it lately, but he hasn't had a reason to. And a lot of reasons not to. Jordan said Sheila used to give her the evil eye, like Jordan was going out with me just to get to Dale or something. Now it's just awkward when she sees her, because of the breakup."

"There's your solution. Convince Dale that Sheila is a witch and trying to cast a spell on Jordan. Baptists don't like witches, do they?" Casey took another bite of her breakfast, which tasted leftover. "Though that could horribly backfire."

"If it worked, yeah, pretty much the backfiring. He would probably storm out and sleep on the lawn until we found a new apartment. Or recite Bible passages until she throws me out by association."

"With my name on the lease," Casey said. "Okay, no witch angle. He could use a normal girlfriend—who's not me."

"I don't know." And it really sounded like he didn't. "He still talks about his spiritual purity and redemption. He really cares about it. It's important to him, and now that he's lost it to Sheila, he might do something crazy. Like lose his faith. Did I tell you he asked her to marry him? That's when she dumped him. Either way, it's depressing. Everyone gets into horrible fights and depressions and feuds because of relationships. Dale is the one guy I know who was, like, above all that. And now this. He really needs to have a great time with a nice girl, no pressure, no judgment."

Casey found herself nodding. The only girls she knew who didn't obsess about guys and get depressed about their dating lives were either ditzy or heavily medicated. "So you're really protecting him, with this date to the honors event."

"Yeah, I guess so. I just want him to remain…I don't know. Dale. He needs his self-respect back. He didn't hold out for marriage like he planned to, and he definitely needs someone better than Sheila to help him get back to normal."

Casey swatted his head, disheveling his curly hair further than it was already disheveled. "Aw. That's so sweet."

"Stop looking at me like I'm a baby kitten."

"Your concerned expression is a good look for you. You should try it around Jordan." She cringed. "Oh, my God. Did I just give my baby brother dating advice? I must be more stressed out than I thought."

"What do you have to worry about?"

"A date for the formal. And don't say his name."

"Dale?"

"No, dork."

It took him a second. "Cappie. Well, he'll be there."

"But not as *my* date. Ashleigh is representing ZBZ by taking our house hasher and I am going solo. Way to make an impression with Panhellenic."

"The only thing I know about the Panhellenic is that it's a group of Greeks arbitrarily judging other Greeks, and that it's a dirty word at Kappa Tau. At least the IFC isn't so strict."

"You can't be surprised by that."

Rusty sighed. "Not really. Why do you care, anyway? Not about going alone, but about what Panhellenic thinks? You haven't recently committed any pranks that almost got you and your whole house suspended." He was referring to the homecoming incident, which had brought a plague on both the houses of Kappa Tau and Zeta Beta Zeta after a few of them had sabotaged the IKI float. Casey was legitimately uninvolved.

"Because my new advisor suggested that working with the council might be a good thing to have on my résumé for a political career. ZBZ has a Panhellenic representative, of course, but I'm wondering if there isn't some way I can get involved."

"Your new advisor? What happened to your old one?"

"I left prelaw and my advisor went with it. The paperwork is still crawling through the gooey muck of the registrar's system, but if it goes through I may be switching to poli-sci."

"Political science? Do you have the credits to graduate on time with that major?"

"If I load up in my final semester, yes. I know Mom and Dad would definitely not appreciate paying for a fifth year. So my academic career is...not in crisis mode...but my social life is."

"I know I sound like a hypocrite for saying this—" because

he had a girlfriend, of course "—but finding the right person is much less important right now. I know you've spent most of college in one relationship or another but…you're a ZBZ and you're good with people. I'm sure you'll find someone eventually."

"Who is not Cappie."

"You know, you're the one who keeps bringing up his name."

Casey finished her croissant with a very unsatisfying munch. "I know. Bad habit. Let's talk about something else. Like…Rob?" She saw him emerge from around the corner of the student center and, upon seeing them, head in their direction.

"You know Robert Howell?" Rusty asked.

"*You* know Robert Howell?"

"He's Dean Bowman's new assistant, and Bowman is, like, obsessed with the engineering event going well. Alumni money and all that."

"I know. About Rob, that is. He came by the ZBZ house with a code of conduct Ashleigh had to sign," she explained quickly. "Hi, Rob."

"Casey, right?" He looked a little hesitant. "I'm here to get some paperwork from Russell, actually. Do you guys—"

"The food order is on my flash drive. My printer is busted," Rusty interrupted. "Casey's my sister. I know we kinda don't look or act alike—"

"You know you can print your paperwork at the student center," Casey said, rather insistently. "That is, if Mr. Howell is willing to wait."

"Please, call me Rob," he said, smiling shyly. "And, yes, I can wait. In fact I'm paid hourly, so take your time."

Rusty jumped up. "Got it. Food order. Printer. I'll be back in a few minutes."

Rob sat down on the bench next to Casey. "So what's going on in the exciting world of ZBZ? Or can you not tell me because of a sorority code?"

"We're not the Amphora Society." At his look of confusion, Casey explained, "It's like Cyprus-Rhodes's Skull-and-Bones, but way more underground and way less threatening. I'm not sure it even exists, but two of my ex-boyfriends spent a huge chunk of time searching for their secret lair."

"I take it they didn't find it."

"It remains a mystery to me to this day," she said. "But ZBZ is not, like, secret. We're just normal girls—hanging out, obsessing about clothing and guys, listening to the pledges complain about mandatory study hours…"

"You're pledge educator?"

"I was pledge educator, then interim president, and now I'm pledge educator again. I don't know when I decided that scheduling was going to be the bulk of my college experience, but here I am."

"You sound…I don't want to say—"

"Depressed? And you're not way off the mark. I love ZBZ, enough to put up with all of the institutional nonsense and over-eager pledges, but I'm a senior. I'm supposed to be cynical about my college experience, thinking of wasted time as the clock ticks down to real life." She added, "Wow, that is depressing."

"It's realistic," Rob said. "A little frustration with the system can spur you to move on to bigger and better things. That's why I left Cornell—it was a bad atmosphere for me. And their political science department was really lacking. Mostly overworked but tenured professors, biding their time until they decide to retire."

"You're poli-sci?"

He nodded. "I was premed for freshman year, I think because my parents wanted it more than I did, and one year of it was enough. I think organic chemistry killed their dream of *Doctor* Howell, M.D. Maybe it was better to have it die early."

"Definitely. I was prelaw for, like...ever. Now I'm doubling up my poli-sci courses to graduate on time and still fulfill my major requirements."

"Prelaws can be pretty crazy."

"You noticed it, too? They all have strange ticks and obsess about scores. Ashleigh said I was dangerously close to looking like one of them."

"What changed your mind? The LSATs?"

"I did okay on the LSAT practice tests," she said, which wasn't a lie. "I even had an interview with Harvard Law. It was going really well, and then he asked why I wanted to be a lawyer, and I realized I didn't have an answer."

"College is supposed to be about figuring out who you are and what you want," Rob said. "Even if it's just girls and beer, as the strong fraternity presence on campus would indicate. At least they're focused on an attainable goal."

"I've never looked at it that way." It was a very philosophical—and kind—way to view drunken frat boys doing body shots off girls' stomachs. "I think the formal will have a slightly different focus."

"Everyone on their best behavior in front of the council and the dean? Yeah, I guess that means no Jell-O shots. Which is a shame, because I really like Jell-O. Not the vodka, necessarily, but the Jell-O."

"You're going?"

"Nah, if Bowman needs me for anything, it'll be the engineering event on Friday."

"Greeks can invite non-Greeks."

"Yeah, like a sorority girl would ask a total stranger." He looked at her. Maybe, finally, he was reading her stare and getting the hint. "Do you…need a date to the formal? I just assumed you had a boyfriend."

She blushed. "If you'd asked a few months ago, you would have been right. But you know, senior year. Cynicism. Changing perspectives," Casey said. "I'm going because I'm pledge educator and I need to support ZBZ, but I am currently dateless."

"Then…may I take you to the formal?" He looked down, his face red. "I feel like I'm in high school, asking for a prom date."

"Formals are a lot like proms. And yes! Yes, totally, you can take me to the prom…er, formal."

His look said, *Really?* but he just stammered, "O-okay, then." They exchanged cell phone numbers. "Great. Awesome." In the distance, they could see Rusty returning, a manila folder in hand. "I don't suppose you know somewhere to rent a tux."

"I'll text you the address," she said, putting on her innocent face for her brother. "Hey, Rus."

"Here you go," he said, turning his attention to Rob, who thanked him and raced off to his next errand. Rusty retook his seat. "So?"

"So what?"

"You have this look on your face like I should ask about something."

There was no reason not to tell him, she supposed. "Rob and I sort of mutually asked each other to the formal on Saturday. I had the invitation and he didn't, but he had to ask. Sort of. You know, as the guy. This isn't Sadie Hawkins Day." On the aforementioned holiday, girls chased around the guys—

literally—that they wanted to date. It was the only time the roles were officially reversed.

"I hope not. Getting chased by my girlfriend is totally not on my list of ideal situations," Rusty said. "She can totally outrun me."

"You were on the track team in high school."

"Yeah, the year that all their first and second picks were disqualified for drinking after an away competition. And it only lasted until the Incident That Shall Not Be Named."

She giggled. Now there was a funny memory. "The one with the hurdles?"

"The Incident That *Shall Not Be Named,*" he said more insistently. "Anyway, Rob seems cool. I don't really know him or anything, but if you need a guy to take you to the formal, I guess it works. And, no, I will not investigate him for you and try to talk him into saying whether he likes you."

"I would never ask you to do that," she said, clarifying with, "*again,* anyway. But it did kind of work."

"And it was kind of embarrassing."

"That, too." She nudged him with her arm. "You're off the hook for this one."

"Oh, my God! He asked you out!"

Excited though she was, Casey felt that not joining in Ashleigh's overexuberance would help to calm her friend down. Casey looked out the window of their shared bedroom instead to avoid Ashleigh's infectious stare. "It was sort of…you know, less direct than that. I did half the work."

"Well, *duh,* you had to. It's completely forgivable. Plus, shy guys? So cute. Especially when they're hot. It's like the perfect mix."

"Ash, he has other qualities," Casey said, feeling compelled to defend Robert as not merely eye candy to hang on her arm. "He's a junior, so he's not too young—"

"Because dating a freshman? Ew—"

"—and he's a political science major, like I hope to be, so we can talk about…political stuff. Course requirements…I don't know. And he's, like, deep. He talks about figuring out who you are and the future, but not the 'we're going to be together forever and ever and our whole careers are planned out' future."

"Yeah, you have a tendency to date guys with plans. Not that it's bad, but it's a little overwhelming. Evan and Max?"

"I think Max's problem was that he *changed* his plans for me and gave up Caltech. And then he brought it up at every possible opportunity even though I never asked him to do it and would have told him not to do it if he had asked." She groaned. "No, no more angsting about Max. Max is gone. Done. Out of my life. Like Evan…and Cappie."

Ashleigh hugged her pillow. "You know, it would be a little more convincing if you didn't get these sad moon eyes every time you said his name."

"Didn't we just go over this?"

"I mean Cappie. Look! I'll get a mirror so you can see."

"I don't need to see it." Casey didn't doubt Ashleigh's judgment on her mood swings when it came to Cappie. They were chronic and terrible and happened way too often. And she didn't even see him that much. "And he'll be at the formal."

"He has to go. He's president of Kappa Tau. Unless there's some medical emergency—"

"He could have a broken leg and he would still go for the free drinks and to say insulting things to someone—Evan, the dean, whoever came his way. And now, probably, Rob."

"Casey, you have to think positive. Maybe he won't come. Or he will and just moon over you in the corner and not bother you or your new awesome, hot boyfriend, who is too cute for words."

"Are you mooning over my date? Which is all he is at the moment. He doesn't count as a boyfriend until the second date, and this isn't even a date. It's a social event. He's *escorting* me."

"In a tux that he wouldn't have to rent if he wasn't taking you. That automatically makes it count as a date."

"Is it weird that we're both going to an All-Greek Formal with non-Greek boyfriends?"

"No," Ashleigh said with a huff. "It just means that the fraternity guys are losers, and we're so over them."

"See? That would be a problem to some people."

Ashleigh rolled her eyes. "People who don't get it. You can't spend time worrying about people who don't get the deeper stuff, Casey. Life's too short. *College* is too short. So he's not in a fraternity. You're setting a good example for your ZBZ sisters."

"You think I am?"

"You made me take Rusty to our formal last year because he had no date, and now I'm president of our house! Not that the two were related. But you see my point. You're showing them that they have options beyond fraternity life, and as much as we ZBZs value our relationships with fraternities, we're empowered women who don't limit our choices because of some arbitrary social code." Ashleigh paused. "Wow. Where did that come from?"

"It was positively presidential," Casey said. "It shows how good you are at your job. It comes to you without you having to think about it. Maybe we should put it in the pledge book."

"Oh, please," Ashleigh said. "Who reads that thing?"

chapter four

When Calvin Owens was a pledge, he'd had to do some disgusting things. Omega Chi Delta liked to keep up the appearance that it was not a bunch of lazy fraternity guys living together, and it did so with pledges. Calvin had used more toothbrushes to scrape floors than he had probably used in his life on his actual teeth. He'd unclogged toilets, trimmed the thorny hedges until his hands bled, and even picked up thirty boxes of pizza, sans car, and delivered them within thirty minutes to his brothers the night before finals. Now that he was an active, it was supposed to be a free ride—provided that he could find a pledge to do the work that needed doing for him.

One particular set of tasks remained. Evan Chambers was his big brother and always would be, and brothers stuck together and helped each other out, even if the situation seemed to be reversed. So when it was time to get Evan out of his drunken stupor and find a tuxedo that would make him look decent when he went to represent the Omega

Chis at the All-Greek Formal, the task fell to Calvin by a massive consensus.

Calvin was smooth. Not overly so, but he had a way of talking with people to calm them down, the very opposite of what his appearance as a built former jock implied. His wide smile showed people how easygoing he was, but he could be angry with his stare if he wanted to be. "Rise and shine, big bro," Calvin said, trying to be cheerful without overdoing it. "You need to get your tux so we can send it for dry-cleaning."

Evan, who was sleeping not in his bed but in the armchair in the billiards room, picked his head up. "What time is it?"

"About five. And if anything doesn't fit, the tailor's closes at six. You haven't gained or lost weight, have you?"

"You can't tell?" Evan wasn't drunk, but he was definitely hungover. Which for him was strange. Or used to be.

It wasn't the first time Calvin had encountered this Evan. In fact, he was witness to the entire slide down the slope from elation to depression. Evan had finally gained access to his trust fund, only to have it come with more strings than a royal marriage alliance. At first he'd tried to buy his happiness about the situation, via Frannie, two new cars and several other women. As Calvin had predicted—and even forewarned his big brother—it hadn't worked. Evan had fought with his parents, he'd fumed and he'd given up his trust fund—and his girlfriend by association, as Frannie was mainly with him for his money and had openly admitted it a few times—in what she no doubt had thought was not an audible conversation—to the entire OX house. Now the mighty Evan Chambers had nothing—except a paid tuition bill, no college loans, a terrific academic record that would easily earn him a scholarship to graduate school, and connections through his fraternity to future job prospects. Really, he had everything anyone would want, if they hadn't just had their multimillion-dollar trust fund taken away. It was all a matter of perspective.

"I don't want to go," Evan announced. Since it was not the first time he'd said it this week, Calvin knew he was referring to the formal.

"Plenty of presidents are going stag or picking up a date on the way. I'm told it's standard procedure for certain fraternities. Psi Phi Pi—"

"They're nerds!"

"Kappa Tau."

"Because Cappie likes to mope in Casey's presence. Wait—she's pledge educator. She might not be there."

"The thing holding you back is *Casey?*"

"No. It's everything, dude."

"Okay, so it's not Frannie, either?"

"Well, Frannie did make things interesting. She sure did know how to wreak havoc in the Greek system." Evan laughed. "Frannie created a whole sorority just to spite Casey. It was maniacal."

"It's supervillain-scale evil, for a sorority sister. I don't think college kids build death rays."

"What are you talking about? Your best friends are engineers." Evan was laughing, which was good. It was still a sickly sort of laugh, and it wasn't very dignified in a bathrobe, but it was better than outright moaning. "But, yes, it was evil on a monumental level. That's how Frannie does things."

"Using evil?"

"Monumentally."

It was enough of a shared laugh to get Evan motivated to

sit up, and then even stand up and contemplate getting dressed. In other words, it was an improvement.

With Calvin's responsibilities to his big brother out of the way, he could finally focus on his own priorities. He looked good in a tux, and he was proud of it. "So. The formal," he said to his roommate and would-be boyfriend, Grant. Yes, it was risky to date a roommate, but their attraction had been unavoidable. *Grant* was unavoidable. "Did you get yours?"

"I don't think I'm going," Grant replied, unusually apathetic about the situation. It was the voice he used when he was trying to dodge something, like an obligation. The look he got from Calvin told him he had to explain himself. "Look, did you go to formals when you were still in the closet?"

"No, but I helped the ZBZs organize a mixer last year."

"Well, I'm just not that kinda guy. Not the organizing part. The going stag because I'm not asking a girl out on a pity date or because I have to so I can keep the image going."

"So you don't want to go stag, and you don't want to go with me."

"Were you really expecting me to go with you? No offense."

Calvin nodded. "None taken." He hadn't even asked. Their relationship was secret, and Grant's sexuality was secret. Calvin had had a hard time being accepted when he came out last year to Omega Chi—actually, Ashleigh had accidentally outed him—and he didn't want to go through that again, or watch Grant go through it, especially when having two guys dating in the house would bring up a host of somewhat reasonable concerns. Never mind that the other guys were so open and obvious about bringing home their girlfriends or the girls with whom they were cheating on their girlfriends. Calvin's previous roommate had been a nightmare of the bed hitting the wall, which had led to the at-first awkward switch to Grant's room. No, hopefully, Grant would come out on his own terms. "I'm used to it. The whole stag thing. Or giving misleading signals unintentionally. Ashleigh once thought I had a thing for her. Before she was president and before I was out, yeah. It was this whole…mess." He didn't want to get into it. He was busy looking for his tie. At least the room was small enough that nothing could get truly lost, though his important items certainly did try. "But you don't have to miss out entirely."

"Miss out on what? They'll be carding, everyone else has a date, and the food will be terrible. I'm not dancing with someone for the sake of it. I'll catch up with you at the after-party."

Calvin frowned, but he knew he couldn't convince Grant to go. To be honest, formals were meant for people who had dates or liked dancing.

"Why are you going?" Grant asked.

"Me? I just like wearing the tux."

"Which tie?"

Rusty groaned as he looked away from his computer screen just long enough to see the ties draped over the unfortunate plaid shirt and corduroy jacket Dale was so enthusiastically holding up. "They're both red. Even I can tell they clash with the jacket. And the shirt. And whatever pants you'll be wearing. And is that a Mickey Mouse tie clip?"

"It's my lucky clip. My grandma Kettlewell gave it to me when I won the second-grade science fair contest, and it's been an upward journey of scientific scholarship ever since."

"Dale, you don't need luck. You're already getting an award. Your grade point average is not changing in the next twenty-four hours." He looked at his watch. "I have to be at the Parkside Hotel in twenty minutes."

"Then pick a tie and you're free to go."

"Fine." Rusty covered his eyes. "The one on the left."

"You have your eyes closed."

"That's exactly my point," Rusty said, throwing on his jacket. "Now excuse me, but I have to go make sure the hotel didn't forget to put out the complimentary fruit platter."

"Wait! You haven't told me who my date is. What if I have to get her a corsage?"

"This is an awards ceremony for good grades, not the prom," Rusty said. "And anyway, it's Casey. If she cared about matching, she would have told you by now."

"Casey?" Dale sputtered. "Your sister, Casey?"

"I don't know any other Caseys." And he didn't have time to deal with Dale's obsessive behavior. He left his roommate in a crush-induced daze—not great, but a definite improvement on leaving him in the lap of cougar Sheila. There was the same amount of drool, but far less swapping of it.

"How do engineers dress, anyway?"

Casey was standing in front of her closet, mindlessly pushing old dresses aside when she answered Ashleigh, "I know how engineers dress. It's more an issue of how their dates dress."

"Oh, my God! You could dress, like, supermodel hot. Don't computer guys date supermodels now and like to trot them out? Like they're getting back at everyone in high school who's now pumping gas?"

"I saw *Can't Hardly Wait,* too," Casey said. "And I don't need Dale any more…excited than he'll already be." Her cell phone rang. "Hello?"

"Hey. Um, hi." It was, of all people, Dale. His voice always squeaked a little when he was nervous. "How...are you?"

She mouthed "Dale" to Ashleigh. "Fine. Just discussing you."

"Really?" He didn't—or couldn't—hide his enthusiasm.

"In direct relation to the awards ceremony."

"Oh. Um. Well." He cleared his throat. "You know that Darwin Lied got permission to play at the after-party? I mean, did you know? Do you know? Can I tell you now?"

"Yes." Casey didn't bother to specify which one of the questions she was answering.

"Um, okay, should I pick you up? Not for the after-party. For the night. I mean the dinner! Not, you know, the whole night. However much you want. You're probably busy. Like later."

"It's on campus, right? Just let me know when it starts and come by half an hour before."

"Awesome! I mean, great. I will be there...at your house, I mean. To pick you up." His voice went to that high pitch again. "Thanks. Um, see you later."

"Bye, Dale." She hung up, the only way to get Dale off the phone. "Maybe I should have asked him what he was wearing."

"What is this event, anyway? How do engineers socialize?"

"By giving each other awards for academic achievement and inviting a bunch of software companies. It's social networking when you don't have a sorority sister to get you an internship somewhere. Rusty said it's alumni and some, like, low-level HR guys scouting the talent."

"So, in a word, *boring,*" Ashleigh pronounced. "At least you can hang out with your little sis. Jordan's going, right?"

"Yeah, and she'll probably be on her own a lot. Rusty's been obsessing about this event forever. And not in a good way. In a planner way." She stopped at an older dress. "No red," she decided, and moved on. "I don't want to look like an accessory. Just because they're engineers doesn't mean I can't be presentable and intelligent and treated as an equal." She thought uneasily of her summer internship with Congresswoman Baker, where she had been regarded as the dumb sorority chick. And the people she'd worked for hadn't even been engineers. They were politicians, and they spoke without using computer acronyms she didn't know. "I need something subtle. Sophisticated. And that matches my eyes."

"So the formal is not a priority?"

"The formal is easy. I have a hot, sexy date. I wear something attractive but not over-the-top. And maybe red." She pulled out a striped gown, black-and-white. "What do you think?"

"The bar code dress? Seriously, you can do better and still not have them drooling over you."

She pulled out another dress, this one green. "Better?"

"Green's good. Neutral. Safe. Environmentally friendly. Wait, is that good?"

"It's green, not tie-dyed." She tossed the dress on her bed. "I'm obsessing too much about this."

"Actually, I think we are dangerously close to obsessing too much about obsessing too much. Which is obsessing…too much."

Casey looked at her best friend. "Green dress?"

"Green dress."

It was almost midnight, and Rusty was ready to eat something, relax and not be obsessed with anything engineering-related for the next twelve hours. The reception at the hotel had lasted longer than he expected, as the alums proved exceptionally chatty, especially the ones who hadn't been on campus in years. Busy answering questions about the engineering program, polymer science and Cyprus-Rhodes in general, he'd only had time to grab a soda and made it last the entire evening.

Seeing his big brother was therefore not ideal, especially when said big brother was perched on his front steps. "Cappie."

"Spitter."

"What are you doing here?"

"I might say the same of you, Sir Hobnobber."

"Well, I live here." And he didn't want to kick Cappie out, but he was sure if he went inside, Cappie would follow.

"Hmm." Cappie just nodded in a conspiratorial manner. He was planning something. "Was it better than clothing shopping with Dale?"

Rusty took a moment to process that. Maybe he was too tired to hear correctly. "What?"

"Your roommate has some serious social impairments. Which is cool. He's developed in other areas. But corduroy? Unacceptable."

"What are you talking about?"

"You told Dale that Casey is his date for the engineering social."

Too exhausted to continue this conversation standing, Rusty dropped his backpack and sat down next to Cappie. "It's not a social, or I guess it is, but yeah. So?"

"So, as you may recall before your Kappa Tau membership threw various female-counterpart opportunities into your lap, some people of…your persuasion—and Dale's—might get a little nervous at the notion of escorting a fine, distinguished woman such as your sister to the event of their semester."

Rusty pondered this for a moment, trying to decipher Cappie-speak. "Did Dale freak out and call you?"

"Your phone was off, and his purity brothers are—"

"On Fire Island, I know." Rusty wasn't sure when the friendship between Dale and Cappie had developed, but it remained as shocking as it had been when he'd first noticed it. Mostly because it was so unlikely. "So you took Dale shopping."

"As I would you, if required to aid in such a noble cause."

"Okay." He knew better than to judge Cappie. "So…why are you still here?"

"Seeing as you are a man of certain influence in the engineering department, or at least in their social planning division, I was thinking that perhaps you would be able to procure an invitation to the aforementioned event."

"For you? Why would you…" This time, he was not so slow on the uptake. "First of all, it's closed to nonengineers to give program members more social time with prospective employers. Second, even if I could get you an invitation, I am not getting you an invite so you can stalk Casey."

Cappie patted him on the shoulder, but it was more of an insistent tug. "Spitter! *Stalk* is such a harsh word."

"It's the only conceivable reason you would want to go to the event. Look, I can bring one guest, and it's Jordan."

"What is this I hear? Do my ears deceive me? Is my little brother failing in his duties to aid a Kappa Tau in distress?"

"You're asking me not to protect my sister from unwanted stress, and to choose between my fraternity and my real obligation to my girlfriend. Who, I might add, actually wants to go for nonstalker reasons."

"That word again! Why do I keep hearing it?"

"Because you're a stalker?" Seeing that Cappie was not ready to give up, and calculating the odds of a healthy Jordan collapsing in the next twenty-four hours, he said, "If Jordan can't make it, you can be my plus one. And no plotting to make sure she can't make it. On this kind of notice, that's all I can offer you."

"Fair enough." Cappie stood up, and they shook on it. "If some predicament were to befall Jordan—completely without my knowledge or involvement, of course—what color tie are you wearing? Or are you wearing the dress and I'm wearing the tie? Color coordination is important."

Rusty rolled his eyes.

Mandatory pledge study hours were over, as was movie night, and the ZBZ house was finally quiet. Fisher had gone home. Aside from the occasional barefoot girl sneaking to the fridge, downstairs was closed up, and most sisters were trying to get some sleep before their Friday classes, if they were foolish enough to take a class scheduled for Fridays.

Casey was not, though she might not be so lucky next semester, if she intended to go through with her poli-sci major. She would need four courses and would be at the mercy of the scheduling program of the university computer system. And she had to pass all of her courses—in some cases, do better than pass—this semester. Casey groaned and threw her textbook on the coffee table.

"Academic distress?" Rebecca Logan's voice was like an uninvited guest at an exclusive party. "The pressures of graduation finally descending on big sis?"

"When did we agree to stop hating each other?"

"I don't recall a formal agreement," Rebecca said, revealing with one hand her real quest—the bowl of popcorn in Casey's lap. "Everything okay?"

"I'll be fine," Casey said. And it was true—she had enough prerequisites to graduate with a few different majors, just not political science yet. Too much of her academic career was dedicated to her then-designated law school destiny. "Not only will my parents not pay for a fifth year, ever since the summer I've had this strange desire to...I don't know..."

"Graduate? Get the hell out of ZBZ?" Rebecca sounded a little too eager at the proposition.

"ZBZ sisters share a lifelong commitment to their friendship and Zeta Beta Zeta," Casey replied. "Something I must have said way too many times as pledge educator—I think I may have actually started to believe it. No, despite my lack of prospective careers or graduate school applications, there is something strangely compelling about not doing the whole college thing again next year."

Rebecca decided to concentrate her efforts on stealing the popcorn by sitting down next to Casey on the couch. "And avoid the Five-Year Frannie stigma."

"It was a stigma way before Frannie. It just sounds better that way because her name starts with an F. There was this Kappa Tau guy, freshman year—he was an active for, like, six or seven years. No...eight. Cappie's big brother, Egyptian Joe."

"A great example, no doubt. I assume Cappie is intending to follow in his illustrious footsteps."

"No." Casey raised her hands. "Or, I don't know. I don't really know what Cappie's deal is right now. Or any guy's deal. I used to have every guy I knew and cared about figured out—and maybe they felt the same way about me. And now there's this..." She gestured to nothing in particular. "And despite being lavaliered by two guys—one who isn't even in a fraternity—I had to scramble for a date to the formal. Totally last-minute."

"At least you have one," Rebecca said, showing a hint of weakness. "Surprisingly, going lesbian for a full week sends the wrong signals to guys."

"Like, 'don't bother'?" Casey asked, and Rebecca nodded ever so slightly. "Yeah, coming out of the straight closet is a way less dramatic gesture. But you're Rebecca Logan—just throw yourself out there. You've never had problems stealing guys from people. Like me." They were at a point in their uneasy friendship where she could finally say it without fear of repercussion. Facts were facts.

"It's not as easy as it looks," Rebecca said, not rising to the bait. "Men are intimidated by female power. A whiff of senatorial fame—however infamous it may be these days—and they flee."

"Trust me, you manage it all by yourself. Not the fleeing guys thing…well, yes, but I meant that as a compliment. Sort of. You can be terrifying. It's a good thing—it makes you look smart. Not a dumb sorority girl."

"Guys like dumb sorority girls," Rebecca said. "*You* have a date." She gave Casey a look that showed she was joking.

"Yeah, and you're not stealing him!" Casey insisted, but without any malice. Yet. "But I did have to go outside the system. He's Dean Bowman's newest assistant."

"Ew."

"Good. Fine. Keep that attitude! Because he's cute and sweet and not a geek or a Kappa Tau and I am *keeping* him. At least for the evening. Hands off Rob."

"Rob who?"

"Robert Howell. Transfer student from Cornell, poli-sci

major. Totally hot and a little shy. And even with the association with Dean Bowman— Rebecca, swallow."

It did look as if Rebecca was going to choke. That was what happened when you inhaled your food midchew, especially popcorn.

"Robert *Howell?* Are you sure?"

"Uh, yes?"

"Brown hair, square face, total hick accent that he covers up a lot?"

"Kinda. I don't have a picture of him—I've met him, like, twice. Do you *know* him?"

Rebecca made an exaggerated noise of disgust. "From, like…when I was young. And stupid. And so was he. He probably still is."

Now Casey was paying attention. "What is it? Is he a jerk? Oh, my God, did you go out with him? I can't believe this!"

"*No.* It was this…thing that totally does not involve dating or college or anything else, if it is really him. And I will go so far as to say that if I implode in his presence, I'm taking people with me."

"Rebecca—"

But Rebecca had lost interest in food or conversation. "It's nothing for you to worry about. Enjoy your date with Robert-freaking-Howell." And she stomped out of the room with all of the indignation possible for someone wearing pink bunny slippers.

"Um, okay." And having nothing else to say, to herself or the empty room, Casey let that stand and retreated to her own bedroom, where Ashleigh was still up. Only her lamp was on, but that was enough for Casey. "Something's up between Rob and Rebecca."

Ashleigh put down her book and turned over. *"What?"*

“Rebecca, like, totally freaked out at his name.”

“Are we talking about the same Rebecca? The one who doesn’t freak out unless there’s a senatorial scandal and a copious amount of alcohol in the vicinity?”

“She did, and she wouldn’t tell me why. Apparently she *knows* him.”

“Okay. Don’t panic. We have, like, two days to find out what it is. Or one, really, if it’s anything. Maybe he dumped her in high school in front of the whole prom or something. Who knows?” She turned back over. “She would have told you if it was anything that would be devastating to you.”

“Ash! It’s *Rebecca*. What am I going to do?”

“I don’t know,” Ashleigh mumbled into her pillow. “Worst-case scenario, we’ll ask her about her dad and put a beer in front of her, and see what happens. It worked when you guys wanted me to spill about Fisher.”

It was cruel, but if it came to it, it would work. And Casey was prepared to make things work.

chapter five

"So then," Ashleigh said as she sat down at the breakfast table with Rebecca and Casey. "What's up with Robert Howell?"

Rebecca gave her a look of disgust, grabbed her bowl of cereal and left the table before Ashleigh even had time to put down her own food.

"Way to go," Casey said. "I was only working on her for, like, twenty minutes!"

"Sorry!" Ashleigh was legitimately apologetic. "Maybe I should put some pledges on it."

Casey played with her spoon, thumping it against the tablecloth. "I think it may be a lost cause."

"Did she say *anything?*"

"In my subtle yet obvious attempts to inquire about her possible history with Rob, I learned that she once attempted to go to summer camp but went home two weeks early because the mosquito bites were ruining her complexion. I now know that she was captain of her varsity field hockey team freshman year after she got the previous captain suspended after finding a sex tape linked to her MySpace page. I've discovered the wonder that is a three-month obligatory playing of the clarinet for a band class requirement, and that her favorite vacation spot is Tahiti because Jamaica is full of guys with smelly hair. But alas, no Rob. And, knowing Rebecca, only the meanest parts of that were true."

"Look on the bright side. If Rob was a serial stalker or weirdo, she would be obligated to tell her big sis about it."

"Or the opposite." Casey softened on Rebecca. Maybe the experience really had been bad—and not relationship related. "It's fine. I've wandered into bad relationships without Rebecca's help before. I can do it again."

"I said *bright* side. Bright side! Don't prejudge Rob because of some snippy comment by Rebecca. I'm sure if he's as bad as she makes him out to be, you'll figure it out soon enough. And then you can publicly ditch him. I bet you can even get her to help."

Casey wasn't so hopeful, or interested in being so hopeful, but she didn't have to respond because her phone rang. More specifically, it chimed. "Rusty, it's nine in the morning and a Friday. What is it?" Actually, the fact that he hadn't run over and intruded throughout the house to tell her about his problem was alarming.

"The engineering awards are canceled for tonight."

"Aw, Rusty! You must be so disappointed."

"This is serious. The visiting alumni got food poisoning from the welcoming party…somehow." The way he said *somehow* was suspicious. "So it's off."

"So I'm off the hook?"

"For tonight. The dean of the engineering department moved it to tomorrow night."

"What?" The sound of her spoon dropping into the empty bowl was apparently quite audible, because almost everyone turned to look at her, and she excused herself to the hallway. "He can't do that! The formal is tomorrow."

"Who do you think reminded him of that?" Rusty said, similarly panicked. "He doesn't care. He said, 'How many engineers are frat guys anyway?'"

"And what was your answer?"

"Something appropriately evasive," he said, as he was probably the only one. "I spoke to my advisor. I spoke to Dean Bowman. I even woke up some people on IFC and Panhellenic and tried to get them on my side."

"What did Panhellenic say?"

"'How many Greeks are engineers, anyway?' And IFC had a few derogatory remarks about the honors engineering program that I will not repeat. Look, we flew in a bunch of alum and some people from technology companies. I just spent an hour on the phone to the hotel, promising them the university would cover their stay for an extra night if they weren't booked there anyway. It's on, and it's on Saturday night."

"Then you have to tell Dale I can't go."

"That is one thing *I* do not have to do," Rusty said defiantly. "It's something *you* have to do. You're the one ditching him."

"You're making Jordan miss the formal!"

"No, I'm not. She can go to the formal without me. I can't make her miss the Greek event of the semester to see some engineers get award certificates. I'll try to join her at the end, depending on how long the ceremony goes. But she's off the hook for the engineering event."

"And so am I."

"Yeah, okay, but *you* have to tell Dale that." He entreated, "Please. You don't know how crazy this has already made me. Just give him a call."

Casey couldn't really refuse. If she did, he would babble for longer than necessary to make her change her mind. "Fine. I'll handle Dale."

"Thank you," he said. "I have to get back to the meeting." And not specifying what the meeting was, he hung up.

"Trouble in Rustyland?" Ashleigh said, appearing in the doorway, and Casey only sighed and closed her phone.

Rusty Cartwright could name, off the top of his head, five days—all within his one year and one semester of college—that were the worst of his life. Certain days of Hell Week made up a few of them, but there was also the day his little brother Andy had depledged, the day Jen K. revealed she was a spy in the Greek system and the day he was duct taped to a wall. Perhaps he was lacking some perspective at the moment, but that Friday morning possibly rivaled all of them. Dale said he was being dramatic, but Dale had gotten more sleep than he had.

The trouble had started at 6:00 a.m., with a call from an alum who now worked in Silicon Valley named Chris McFadyen. Chris had his cell phone number, as Rusty had chatted him up the previous night out of interest in his work in biopolymers, polymers that were produced by living organisms. It was a hot field because of the green movement and the move toward environmentalism in the hard sciences, even ones involving plastics like polymers, but that wasn't why McFadyen was calling. He'd had less sleep than Rusty, having been up all night bowing to the porcelain goddess, and said he might not be able to make the event if he didn't start holding down liquids and maybe solids in the next twelve hours. Rather politely he sent his regards.

The next call came twenty minutes later, from a second recipient of Rusty's cell phone number, Eric von Riegers, asking if he knew where in town he could find some Pepto-Bismol. He was considerate enough not to ask Rusty to get it himself. Rusty checked his Google maps and directed him to a nearby CVS. Eric also apologized profusely for his possible inability to attend the event that night.

Then a call came in on the main house line. Dale took it, and immediately handed it off to Rusty as though the phone was covered in biohazardous waste. It was Devora Kessin, associate dean of the engineering department, and she was calling from the emergency room, though she said she was about to be transferred to a regular floor. She sounded astoundingly composed for someone with mercury poisoning.

At which point, Rusty began to suspect something.

The caterer didn't answer the phone. Rusty wrung his hands for another few minutes before the next call came, this one from the dean of engineering. Rusty's presence was requested—*demanded*—at his office, pronto. He barely had time to get his clothing all buttoned and tucked in before appearing in the dean's office, where a pink bottle of Pepto-Bismol, half-emptied, was rather prominently displayed on the desk. Rusty's advisor, Dr. Hastings, actually showed up, as well, his face rather ashen, as the dean began going down the list and calculated that sixty-three percent of the invited guests of Cyprus-Rhodes currently staying at the Parkside Hotel had called in with what was definitely some form of food poisoning. Fortunately for Rusty, inquiries were not made as to why he had selected that caterer and that menu. There were too many logistics to be handled, some of them by Rusty himself. The dean was either too distracted by illness or uninterested in Rusty's incompetence, as he selected *him* to locate a new caterer immediately, and money was no object when it came to safety ratings.

"We'll recover the money in the lawsuit, I'm sure," the dean said, planning revenge on the caterer before making use of his garbage can for something other than paper waste. As to Rusty's question of how he was supposed to find a caterer in less than twelve hours, the dean's answer—when he recovered—was simple. "The event has been moved to tomorrow night. Attendance will suffer, but we'll extend the rooms at the hotel for an additional night. It's the only thing we can do without canceling altogether."

"But, sir, the All-Greek Formal—"

"Is what?" The dean betrayed not a hint of patience.

"Is tomorrow night."

The dean exchanged looks with Dr. Hastings, to which their response was a joint shrug.

"Locating a facility to host won't be a problem. Dean Bowman understands the importance of alumni contributions. Besides, how many engineers are frat guys, anyway?"

Released from the meeting, Rusty called what would almost assuredly be a friendly voice. "Hey, Jordan." He knew it was not too early for her, as she had a 9:00 a.m. class.

She answered in a rather perky voice, even for her. "Hey, Rus! What's up?"

"A lot of alumni's stomachs," he answered before he stopped himself. "I suspect undercooked fish."

"What, did they have you running to CVS?"

"Practically. I mean no, they didn't actually make me do that, but I just got back from a meeting with the dean." He swallowed. "The event is moved to tomorrow night."

"Oh, no!"

"I know. Look, you're off the hook for the awards, obviously. I can't ask you to miss the formal. Just try not to pick up any cute guys from a more distinguished fraternity while I'm not there to try to punch them and then get my butt kicked."

"Rus, I would never do that to you. Plus, who would I go for, an Omega Chi? Ew!"

"You're a ZBZ. That's the opposite of what you should say."

"Yeah, and how well do I fit in at ZBZ?" It was true. Without Casey's constant support, tinged with a hint of desperation—Casey didn't handle failure well—Jordan probably would have depledged the first week, or not pledged at all. She was the very opposite of the ZBZ image of a perfect girlie girl. Her destruction last week of her pink bunny slippers, a gift to all pledges, via a washing machine accident that might well have been intentional, was a testament to that. Now the slippers looked like little demon cats, all red and eyeless and with torn-off ears, thanks to her not using the gentle cycle. Rusty had won significant points by saying it was an improvement on her evening footwear. Jordan continued, "Do you want me to ditch?"

"No! Totally go to the formal. You probably already have a dress."

"I can return it. I haven't worn it outside the dressing room, and it still has the tags. Although, it actually isn't as uncomfortable as I assumed it would be. Mostly because I refused to get anything with itchy lace and matching heels."

Rusty actually shivered at the idea of Jordan in lace. "I might make it. It depends if I can leave the engineering event early. But I have to be there, at least for the opener, to make sure things go well."

"Like you did last night?" She chuckled.

"Yeah, exactly. It's weird—like they totally forgot who chose the caterer. I think it's that the dean is as sick as everyone else. Must have been the breaded salmon. I saw *everyone* eating that."

"Gross."

"I know. Hence, my good health." He sighed. "Look, I'm really sorry to miss the formal. You want to get together tonight? Apparently I'm free."

"Sure. Anything going on at Kappa Tau?"

"By virtue of it being Friday, I'm sure there's something going on. Not that the concept of a weekend is a lot different from a weekday to most actives. Besides, Cappie— Oh, crap! Cappie!"

"What about him?"

He put a hand over his eyes. "You have *no idea*."

"I have to say, Spitter, you do not disappoint," Cappie said, somehow towering over a nervous and exhausted Rusty, even though he was slumped on the couch and Rusty was sitting up. "Poisoning an entire guest list is a little extreme, but considering the nobility of your quest, the means to your end can certainly be excused."

"I didn't know the fish was bad. Or maybe it wasn't even the fish," Rusty said. "Maybe it was the fruit provided by the hotel. I don't know."

"I, for one, make it a habit not to include a lot of dangerous fresh fruit in my diet," Cappie said. "But really. Going all of this way just to fulfill a promise to your big brother and conveniently not have to shun your girlfriend? Exemplary for a pledge, extraordinary for an active. I'm almost tempted to hug you."

"Please don't," Rusty said, knowing Cappie actually wouldn't, because it would require him getting off the couch. "I only said you could go if Jordan couldn't because I thought that was impossible."

"The odds were for you, but fate was against you. A fate designed to get me an invitation to the exciting engineering awards ceremony. Is it even a ceremony? Or just hobnobbing with people who edit Wikipedia for a living?"

"Hey! You have to go to the formal. You can't play sick if you're at another event."

"Unlike certain other people in this room, I may have made contingency plans," Cappie answered. "In the event that I am unable to fulfill my presidential duties on Saturday night by appearing at the formal, a certain someone will take on the responsibilities—and title—of Kappa Tau president for the hours in question. And that person is..." He looked around, then under the cushions. "And that person is whoever's name comes out of the fishbowl. Spitter, some help here?"

A quick search of the main room revealed a dry fishbowl, still with the colored rocks and plastic treasure chest at the bottom, filled with people's names on slips of paper. "And the president of Kappa Tau for the duration of the All-Greek Formal is—" Cappie did nothing if not dramatically "—Heath. I'm sure he'll do us proud."

"Is my name in there?"

"Yes, but your prior obligations—mainly, being my date to the engineering event—would disqualify you." He put the fishbowl back in its spot behind the broken lamp.

"You're only going to stalk my sister."

"You are so judgmental when you're cranky. I have to admit, not one of your better qualities. Have some faith, little bro. Could it be that I have other—perhaps even a litany—of reasons for wanting to attend such a prestigious event?"

"Name one."

Cappie put his hand around Rusty's shoulders. "Perhaps I want to spend some time with my fellow engineering majors? A position I held for two days, admittedly, but we bonded a lot during those two days."

"You were an engineering major for two days? Why?"

"I was young, foolish, and thought that there was a class on how to build a hovercraft open only to majors. But alas, none was offered. Ever since, Kappa Tau has had to make due with the G.I. Joe inflatable set I got off eBay."

"We have a G.I. Joe hovercraft?"

"We *had* a G.I. Joe hovercraft. And lost many a brave plastic soldier upon discovering that it doesn't work very well in a tub of beer."

"So you're taking Cappie?" Jordan asked. They were sitting on the Kappa Tau roof, enjoying the sunset after a long day of arrangements and other hassles for Rusty, to be followed by an open night, thanks to some bad fish. "Did he have some excuse or is he just chasing after your sister?"

"He said he was an engineering major for two days."

"So?"

"Exactly. But I promised him he would be my backup if you couldn't come—not figuring massive food poisoning into the plan—and I have to keep my promise."

"I don't have to go to the formal."

"You are not going to miss a Greek event for me. Especially the All-Greek Formal. Your pledge sisters will be talking about it for days. I can't do that to you," he said. "Besides, I haven't told Cappie yet, but Casey will probably break her date with Dale to go to the formal. *She's* not going to miss out on the event of the year."

"She is kind of…Super Sorority Sister. If that was an action hero, she would totally be it. But what's she going to say to Dale?"

"I left that up to her."

"Aw, Dale will be crushed."

"I know. And then so will Cappie when he actually *does* have to make conversation with engineering students. Maybe I should tell him. I would, but then he'll just go to the formal and do what he was planning to do anyway—publicly moon over Casey and then ruin her date. And possibly get in a fight I won't be there for."

"I have a camera on my cell phone."

He turned his head sideways to face her. "I love you."

"For my camera or for me?"

"Depends on the megapixels on the camera," he said, not meaning it at all, but she knew that, and kissed him.

Casey Cartwright looked down at her cell phone for the third time in the last minute. The contact number on the screen cried out to her with its tiny blue light, reminding her and scaring her at the same time. It was Friday night, well after classes, and now she had no excuse not to call. Soon, perhaps, it would be too late to call, and she would have that excuse until tomorrow morning.

"If I tell him in the morning, he won't cry himself to sleep tonight," she reasoned, and turned to her laptop to continue her paper, then back to the phone. "It's the right thing to do."

Ashleigh, fresh from dinner and a movie with Fisher, entered the bedroom. "Um, don't you have somewhere to be?"

"You are not kicking me out for Fisher. House rules. And friend rules."

"I mean, hello, engineering event you've been obsessing over?"

Talking to Ashleigh at least gave her a reason to close the phone and turn away from it, which she welcomed. "It was postponed."

"Okay."

"To tomorrow night. Food poisoning. Rusty didn't know not to go with the lowest bidder for the catering."

"But...we'll all be at the formal."

"And the deans assumed...mostly correctly...that not many honors engineers with a 4.0 grade point average were invited to an All-Greek Formal. Rather than have the alumni fly back in on the university dime, they decided to just hold it the same night."

"So you're out of your date with stalker Dale?"

"He's not a stalker," Casey admitted, because it was true. "He just has a crush on me, but it's not like he follows me around or anything. This was going to be huge for him, I'm sure. I'm going to break his heart."

"So, duh, have Rusty tell him. Aren't they roommates? It's not like they don't see each other."

"Rusty said it's my responsibility to let Dale down, and he's right. I made the promise. I should be the one to break it." She picked up her phone. "Is a text message good enough, or is it even worse?"

"You're not dating him. You're not actually going out with

anyone yet—except supercute Rob, whom you will not be going out with if you miss your first date with him. Rob has potential. He's cute and you said he's smart—"

"I know."

"And he's a poli-sci major so you guys can talk about...that. What are you going to talk about with Dale?"

"Well, most of the time when we're in the same room, he clams up."

"See? And then there's Panhellenic, which for some reason you've been going on about..."

"I just wonder if I should somehow get involved in Panhellenic. It would help me network at Nationals and be good for my postcollege résumé. Or so says Congresswoman and ZBZ sister Paula Baker."

"The woman who gave you that internship?"

"I may have had a terrible time, but I don't question her career judgment. So, yes, important social event plus hot guy should win over sisterly duty."

"And you have the perfect dress for it."

"And I have the perfect dress. But...I promised Dale first. What should I do?"

Ashleigh huffed. "Uh, lame-ass engineering event with stammering guy and your brother or the Greek event of the year? Plus, new guy who is not weird or an engineer stalking you or a previous boyfriend? Plus, networking opportunities? You owe it to yourself to go to the formal. There's not really any...I don't know, *decision* to make here."

The phone still in her hands, Casey squeezed it. "You're right."

"Of course I am!" Ashleigh was way too enthusiastic about it.

Casey was not so sure. "I'll tell him in the morning. So he doesn't have to be upset tonight."

"Yeah, and where is he going to find a date at this hour? Plus none of them will measure up."

Maybe she would tell him at the last minute, when he was too panicked about the actual event to further panic. "However I tell him, it has to be smooth. Appropriate. Kind." And however it was done, one thing was certain—it could be done tomorrow.

chapter six

Casey checked her phone one more time, then focused her attention on the mirror and the pledge at her side. "You seriously have no makeup?"

"I had some, but it expired," Jordan said. Her gown was amazing, sparkling blue to match her eyes, and there was a napkin around her neck to protect it from any makeup-related disasters. "Did you know it's only good for five years?"

"Then you just have a natural complexion that people would kill for," Casey said to her little sis. "Nothing that can't be enhanced."

"Why am I doing this again?"

"Because being beautiful is not just about looking hot and having guys fall all over you. It's about self-esteem and presenting the best of yourself. You're a ZBZ—you are not expected to look your best all the time. You just *do*."

"A paradigm of womanhood?" Jordan smirked.

"I have other things to do," Casey said, adding, "though helping out my little sis is always the most important. Now, red or pink lipstick? I'm thinking something subtle, because of the color of your dress."

Jordan managed to control her gag reflex through the entire procedure, which took longer not because of her indecisiveness but because she deferred all opinions to Casey, who insisted she make her own choices. When the work was finally done, she was amazing—radiant, really—but nothing Casey could say could really convince Jordan of that, and she thanked her and scampered away, Rebecca passing her on the way.

"Big problems with little sis number two?"

Now Casey had to control her gag reflex. "You know how pledges are. Especially ones I seem to be in charge of," she said, in reference to Rebecca's near disastrous pledge year.

Rebecca took her place in front of the mirrors. She didn't have much makeup to put on, but she needed no instruction, and she spent a lot of time getting it perfect—something Casey was familiar with. And since Rebecca was solo—as far as Casey knew, and didn't want to bring up—she was putting on an extra shine.

"So am I really going into this thing without you revealing the mysterious past of the infamous Mr. Howell?"

"Yes."

"Did you date him and he dumped you in public?"

"No."

"Did he work for your father?"

Rebecca grimaced. "No." But her face said that touched a nerve.

"Does he have photos of you during your fat years?"

"I did not have 'fat years,'" Rebecca said with all the self-confidence that would make one assume that she truly hadn't and had no reason to lie. Of course, Rebecca always sounded that way, even when she was lying through her teeth. "Though remind me to bring that up in the next game of 'I never.' I would find that interesting."

"Did he humiliate a young, impressionable Becca Logan at summer camp?"

"You already asked that one."

"Did you have a crush on him?"

"Try again."

Casey closed her case of blush with an extra-hard snap created by indignation. "You know it's your sisterly duty to inform me if I'm walking into a disaster zone. I would do the same for you, if you didn't go ahead without telling us first."

"Just keep him away from me, and you'll be fine," Rebecca said, not so reassuringly. "If he knows what's good for him, that shouldn't be hard." With that vague warning, she left.

Casey was still cleaning up—a clean house was a well-run house—when Ashleigh entered. "Which situation should I ask about first?"

"Dale's taken care of. I left two messages on his voice mail and sent him a text. What more can he ask?" Casey checked her phone again. "No response. He must be really upset."

"He'll get over it. What did Rebecca say?"

"That she never had fat years, and nothing else."

"Ooo, this gets juicier by the minute."

"Maybe not. Maybe it was something not dating related that she's still upset about. Or maybe he's grown up and is simply the sweet, hunky guy I've met and invited to the formal."

Ashleigh shrugged. "Where there's smoke, there's fire."

"Are you trying to sabotage my date?"

"I'm just looking out for you. Which Rebecca apparently isn't doing."

"Surprise, surprise."

Ashleigh qualified it with, "If it was really terrible, she would say something. So just chill, go to the formal with your new hotness monster, and maybe it'll all come out in some dramatic moment that everyone remembers for years." She continued, "Ew, that didn't sound good. I meant for it to sound better."

"I know you did. And I am probably overthinking this because I met a new guy and he's not a Greek and I don't know anything about him and he's not—"

"Cappie. Or Max. Or Evan. Or even the original hotness monster."

"Right. Exactly. So I need to just...relax."

Casey succeeded in taking her mind off it, sort of, by giving the speech to remind pledges to be on their best behavior in front of the other Greeks and especially members of the Panhellenic board, who would be there. She tried to do so without making too many references to their disastrous newspaper exposé and the horrible restrictions on campus life that had followed, and the pledges seemed to get the point. Either they were antsy by the end of the speech or some of them just weren't so used to heels and needed to sit down, because they were squirming.

Then it was time to go. Some of the sisters were picked up by their dates, and some had to make their own way to the formal. The pledge class went together, and Casey saw them off from the porch. Most of her sisters had left when Rob appeared, almost a phantom in the night in his black tux on the poorly lit streets—the university was trying to save energy—but his smile lit up the night, or at least her night. "Hey," he said, a little bit nervously.

"Hey," she replied, standing gracefully, or trying to. The responsibility to her sisters sometimes left her feeling like a mother hen.

"What's bringing you down? Or am I reading you wrong?"

"Just making sure my little sisters find their way," she said. "Kind of leaves me the last woman standing."

"I thought the president went down with the ship?"

"Ashleigh's the president, so she's supposed to get there early and stay through to the end. Also, her date lives ridiculously close to the university ballroom, and she is therefore picking him up. They've been dating for a while, so she doesn't expect any dramatic, romantic gestures like Fisher arriving on his motorcycle to take her."

"Should I have been dramatic?" he said. "Because a horse and carriage is really expensive. I checked."

She accepted his hand. "I'll manage without the dramatic gestures tonight, thank you. In fact, I would appreciate a lack of them." He had no idea how close that comment had struck to a previous formal-transportation disaster. Max had been romantic and dramatic....

Walking close together, they headed in the direction of the main campus, where student cars were not allowed without a special permit that neither of them had.

"So," Rob said, his hands in his pockets, possibly a sign that he didn't know where to put them. Maybe he was nervous because he liked her? "You're not a big romance type? I sort of had you pegged differently."

"When it's good, it's good. When it's bad, it's very bad. And awkward. And then you break up with the guy because he's creeping you out. Or he's overcompensating because he's a mess and he doesn't know what to do with his life." She frowned. "Wow. Bad way to start the evening."

"A nice walk?"

"My dating history. Forget what I said." She took his arm.

"Tonight is fresh and new and all about new beginnings. Or just an open bar and schmoozing with Panhellenic."

He laughed. "If you want. I haven't found them that interesting. Mostly administrative. They have a lot of memos to be copied."

"My recent interactions with them have been when my house has done something wrong," she said. "Which, admittedly, has only partially been on my watch."

"I read about last year."

She stopped. "You did?"

He smiled to reassure her. "Yeah, having wild parties and fooling around on campus? Who knew? I was wondering why everyone was so scandalized. I've seen bigger scandals in 1950s educational films, though those scandals are usually everyone rushing off to get married without their parents' permission. If Cyprus-Rhodes doesn't want to admit it's a normal university, then it has a serious complex about itself."

"Really?"

"Really. Maybe it would have been scandalous if this was a Mormon campus, where guys have mandatory haircuts and the vending machines don't sell soda with caffeine. But we're in college. Glorified summer camp," Rob said, and they continued walking. "I think the reaction was because, you know, they had to react like it wasn't the status quo because then it would be like they were saying it's okay. It's all about presentation—especially for the alumni. Dean Bowman is serious about how we look to the alumni, especially the ones who can't seem to remember what *they* did in their campus days. Speaking of which, I've heard legends around the office about Dean Bowman's wild years as an undergrad."

"I thought those were rumors. Or something Cappie made up."

"Who's Cappie?"

"The president of Kappa Tau." She grimaced. "And I might as well just tell you—my ex-boyfriend from freshman year."

"The president of Kappa Tau? That's not the name on the info at the registrar's office."

She stopped dead and faced him. "You know Cappie's real name? Oh, my God, you can't tell anyone."

"No worries. Student confidentiality and all. Seriously, I need this job. It's the reason I had such an easy time with transferring my credits and my source of housing."

"Seriously. You have to keep it a secret."

"I don't remember it, anyway. I just remember it was weird, and his file in Dean Bowman's office is huge."

She patted him on the arm. "You know, I'm starting to think you're a really great guy."

Dale knew he was late. Far too late. He arrived at the ZBZ house running, huffing because his tie was too tight for this kind of physical activity. Approaching the ZBZ house was always a little intimidating, but it was Dale's responsibility to pick Casey up. Worse, she didn't even know what time he was coming.

Casey did not answer the door. It was someone he didn't know, in a bathrobe. He wasn't that late, was he? "Um, hello?" she said.

"Hi. I'm here…to pick up Casey." He tried to catch his breath without leaning over or possibly collapsing on the front steps. "She's expecting me. But maybe she isn't. I was going to call her but the phone company repairman for the house line didn't show—"

"Uh-huh."

"—and my cell phone, okay, it doesn't hold up to water. It's dead. I tried to call to give her a time, but I couldn't. So I thought maybe I could e-mail her, but the phone company is owned by the cable company and they said the reason they couldn't send the repairman was because he was busy fixing the cable lines for Internet—"

"Uh-huh."

"—and if we had only stayed on campus, we could have reliable service! Except for that time it went down because someone overloaded the campus server trying to download every *Star Trek* episode ever made in HD format—"

"Uh-huh."

He pushed his glasses back up on his nose. "I think he got halfway into *Next Generation*. Anyway, so everything was down and Rusty was already gone so I couldn't reach her and I figured I would go over early, but band practice was held up—do you know we're playing tonight? Anyway I think my watch is slow. I should have gone digital but it was my grandfather's watch."

"Uh-huh."

"So, I tried to take the campus bus and the times posted are *completely* wrong. No wonder I've never taken them—"

"Uh-huh."

"And…wait, am I at the right house?" He thought maybe there was no way he could panic more, but maybe he could.

"Oh. Yeah. I'm Betsy." She closed her robe tighter as if she was suddenly self-conscious, even though it didn't truly need closing. "I'm a ZBZ. But I didn't have a date. Or a dress."

"Okay." He was confused by her air of befuddlement. Maybe she just didn't understand how critical this moment was. "Where's Casey?"

"She left. For the thing."

"Oh." He frowned. "At least she won't be late. Thanks!" Without spending more time while his date was waiting, he took off in the direction of the social hall. Maybe his luck was finally changing.

"Professor Hale—nice to see you. Yes, I was in your class last semester. Third row. Great TA. Mr. McFadyen—thank you for coming. I hope you're feeling better." Rusty's current job as he stood by the trimmed hedges leading to the cocktail hour outside the meeting hall was supposed to be checking invitations, but was turning into more of a greeter job, as his advisor had given him specific instructions to record who, of the alumni and professors stricken by the mysterious illness, actually showed up. He even had a clipboard. Fortunately he was good with names and faces, and knew most of the professors anyway. "Professor Girard. How are you?"

"Please, it's Nick." The paleontology professor shook his hand. The event was open to all professors, though few outside of the hard sciences attended. Rusty had taken Girard's class for a social sciences credit first semester. "Is it me, or do these things get bigger every year?"

"I think it's more for the alumni than the students being honored."

"And the job market. You youngsters need those connections. I'm just here to see some old students."

"Well, enjoy."

Professor Girard nodded and entered. Next up was Associate Dean Devora Kessin, still pale from her adventure in mercury poisoning. "What's the ice sculpture this year?"

"A satellite."

"Last year it was a swan. Lazy sculptors."

He nodded and felt his phone vibrate. It was Jordan texting him. Rather than spend all the time it would take typing, he ducked behind the bushes and called her. "Hey."

"Hey, yourself. How goes?"

"Not bad. I think it was, like, a twenty-four-hour thing. Everyone seems pretty recovered."

"Where's your Man-Date?" Jordan asked.

"Cappie's not here yet. I mean, if he is coming. I didn't tell him Casey was going to the formal instead, but he might have figured it out."

"Aw, your loyalty is cute. What about Dale?"

"I haven't seen him. I'm stuck at the entrance for alumni and professors. Students go in the other door. Did Casey let him down easy?"

"She sent him a bunch of messages. He hasn't called or written back."

"That's weird." It didn't seem like Dale, but Rusty couldn't answer for his whereabouts. He'd been too busy and hadn't seen him all day. "I miss you. How's the formal?"

"I don't know. The pledges are going together, but we got held up by a stocking emergency and we're at the campus drugstore. Not very formal."

"If I can get out of this thing, I promise you I will."

"You should stay. Make contacts. Get deans to like you." She was really trying to be encouraging. "Enjoy."

"Talk to you soon." He hung up in time to greet his advisor. "Professor Hastings."

"Mr. Cartwright." He always called people by their names in a way that seemed calculated to make them flinch. "How is our attendance looking?"

"Not so bad. Most of the people who got sick yesterday are already here. Everyone else is straggling in."

"And the caterer?"

"I specifically told them 'no fish,' and they came very highly rated by the president of the university." That had been a very awkward call. "So, okay, I think."

His advisor actually showed a hint of a smile. "Good job, Cartwright. Keep your grades up, and you may well be just *attending* next year."

A backhanded compliment if he'd ever heard one. Rusty just said, "Thank you, Professor."

Rusty was watching his advisor turn around the corner when someone said from behind him, "Jerkwad."

"Hey, Cappie."

"Just because you can't say it doesn't mean I can't, despite my great esteem for the professors of the engineering department," Cappie said. He was dressed appropriately for the event, which was not black tie but still quite formal.

"Students are supposed to go in the other side."

"I am not a student. I am either a connoisseur of the hard sciences or your date. Pick one."

Rusty rolled his eyes, but he had to be honest with his big brother, now that he was facing him. "You know, I heard Casey is going to the formal instead. ZBZ responsibilities and all."

"That's sad," Cappie said with remarkably little remorse. "And if my sole intention in attending this fine event was, as you say, to stalk Casey Cartwright, then I would be quite disappointed and tempted to desert you and relieve Heath of his presidential duties at the formal. But, as I have always maintained, your sister's well-being is not my only concern in life." He said it so smoothly that it almost sounded true.

"So you're avoiding the formal."

"Spitter, you're so quick to judge sometimes."

"You are *totally* avoiding the formal."

Cappie rather hesitantly nodded. "Rebecca's been texting me all day to be her date."

"Rebecca? As in Rebecca Logan? Did you get back together—"

"No. The answer is no, but her messages were insistent. Whatever her scheme is, I would much prefer the comfort of the warm bosom of engineering—"

"Please never say that phrase again—"

"—to suiting her needs at the formal. I'll take my chances with the poli-science—"

"Polymer science—"

"—majors. Thanks for the invite." He patted Rusty on the back, then strutted in as only Cappie could, as if he owned the place.

"Remind me why I'm doing this."

Calvin barely held back the mandatory eye roll that now came so often when dealing with Evan, as he entered to find, with some surprise, Evan perfectly dressed for the formal. Giving up your trust fund apparently didn't affect your ability to properly position a cummerbund. "Because you're president of Omega Chi."

"Yeah, and?" Evan did not sound convinced.

"It's your IFC duty, and you want the house to look good in front of Panhellenic." Everyone knew that, when it came to the Greek system, the Panhellenic organization, which handled sorority issues, wielded more power, if only by virtue of their seriousness, than the far more easygoing Inter-Fraternity Council.

"Yeah, and?"

"And because you're tired of being a wuss."

"Okay, good enough." Meaning, it was enough to inspire Evan to leave his room. "You going stag?" Evan generally didn't ask about Calvin's current status, which all things considered was very understandable.

"Yeah. Currently am." Actually, Calvin had given up on his Dale-inspired purity pledge and was now with his roommate, Grant, but he could tell Evan was not in the mood for a chat about his personal life. "I heard my ex is standing in as Kappa Tau president."

"Why? Cappie would never miss an open bar. Is he avoiding someone?"

"You know, avoiding your ex is not the only reason someone would want to miss a formal. There's the tux, the crushing boredom of formality, the distinct possibility of embarrassing yourself and therefore your house in front of Panhellenic—"

"Which some of us excel at," Evan said. "But if Cappie's not there..."

"Or Rusty." Rusty's public brawl with Evan from back when Evan had been caught cheating on Casey was still legendary.

"Rusty's not going?"

"He has some honors engineering event that his advisor is making him help with."

"Sucks."

"I know. So really, we're the lucky ones."

"No Cappie, no Rusty, no Frannie. Trying to keep the drama to a minimum might be easier than I thought." He stopped on the sidewalk. "Or not."

With her extremely nice and expensive automobile behind

her and her floor-length gown, Rebecca Logan looked as if she'd stepped right out of a car commercial. Or a champagne commercial.

"Calvin," Rebecca said, and it was hard to tell whether she was angry or not because she was so good at being politely dismissive. Calvin shot Evan a supportive look, but his ability to prop up his big bro did not extend into Logan territory.

Evan exhaled, waiting until Calvin and any other frat brothers were well out of earshot. "So…what did I do?"

"I need a favor."

He held up his hands. "You know that I'm broke these days."

"Do I look like I need money?" But then her facial expression actually softened—for Rebecca. "I need a date."

"With me?"

"It's only for the length of the formal, and any after-party that we mutually agree to attend."

He cocked his head. "What's the catch?"

"No catch. Unless you consider being driven by a girl to the formal and not the other way around as a catch."

"Okay, now I *have* to know the catch."

Rebecca hesitated. "There's this guy."

"Do I know him?"

"No. He's a transfer student working for Dean Bowman named Robert Howell."

"That guy? He came by with a list of rules of behavior for the formal."

"Uh, yeah. He did that for everyone. He's Casey's date."

"And?"

"And I hate him. For reasons that are not what you're immediately thinking. I haven't seen him in years."

"Do you want to disclose those reasons?" Evan asked.

"No. I want to go to the dance and not be annoyed by him or the presence of him or the pledges obsessing about it since I mentioned he was a scumbag. So can you just...escort me? Knight in shining armor?"

"Not if I have to fight some random guy and I don't know why."

"You don't have to fight him," she said.

"That's what knights do. Fight people. And...dragons, I guess. Look, what is this about?"

"Me asking you for a favor," she said.

"And why me?"

"Because I would rather hang out with you than anyone else there tonight."

The problem was it actually sounded legitimate. It actually sounded as though Rebecca Logan, political and social wonder woman, needed help—*his* help. And she looked pretty hot in that dress. Evan sighed. "Fine, but at the end of the night, you have to tell me what this is about."

"Or get you drunk enough that you forget."

He was open to possibilities. "Either one."

chapter seven

Casey and Rob arrived at the formal fashionably late, which was precisely on time for both of them. Ashleigh was already there of course, with Fisher hovering nearby but never straying far from the sushi bar. Most of the pledges were there, too, either with their dates or staying together looking giggly and nervous. The evening was excessive even by Greek standards, as a number of deans were in attendance. It was a bit like a prom, but without teenagers sneaking out the back to smoke joints in the parking lot. There was also serious carding, which meant a lot of people's long champagne glasses were filled with bubbling cider, but it was a good presentation. The theme was white, or at least the drapes were, and all of the balloons and decorations. It was either supposed to be romantic or the university had skimped on the Greek budget and had old tablecloths bleached. Only the dance floor had some color, if black checkerboard counted as a color. Either way, it looked nice.

"Too bad your boss isn't here," Casey whispered as they

entered without incident. "The Greeks are on their best behavior."

"Dean Bowman at a Greek formal?" Rob laughed in a nice way. "That'd be fun to see. But the engineering event is of course more important to him, because of the alumni attendance. Also, I think the university's trying to talk up their scientific departments to the whole college world." The mention of the engineering awards pained Casey, who tried not to flinch. "What is it?"

"Nothing." She smiled, though it was superficial. "I definitely need a drink."

"And I just passed the big two-one. Can I get you something?"

This time her smile was real—and gracious. "Thank you." She dispatched him with a drink order, fumbled with her purse to make sure it was hanging appropriately from her shoulder and joined the pledge group. "So how are you? Not that you should be way different from half an hour ago."

There was some talk of dresses, of course, as it was the first thing anyone talked about, aside from who showed up with whom.

And then, the defunct IKI sisters arrived.

People almost didn't notice, as many of them had legitimate reasons to be there with their still-Greek dates, but a few were there not of their own standing. The sisters themselves were no longer Greeks, but a few seemed to have slipped in anyway and immediately made their way to the bar. The IKI sisters were making fools of themselves but didn't seem to know it.

Casey kindly reminded her snarky pledges—*kindly* being the operative word—that, "Some of the IKI sisters were originally ZBZ sisters."

"But they left!"

She sighed. "They didn't mean to. Sort of. It's complicated." Seeing they weren't satisfied by that, she added, "We might one day welcome them back to ZBZ—and forgiveness is a sisterly virtue." She left the pledges with that, this being a formal and not a house meeting, and they would just continue when she was gone.

Realizing one pledge was missing from the group, Casey looked around and found Jordan texting on her phone in a corner. "Hey."

Jordan looked up. "Hey." Despite her position, she did not sound overly distressed or bored—yet. "Rusty says hi."

"How's the engineering event going?"

"Their ice sculpture is way better than ours. He sent me a picture." She glanced at the ice roses melting at the cocktail table now on the other side of the dance floor, impressive in their own right. "At least it's not a swan."

"You know, Jordan, there *are* benefits to the formal. Mainly, gossip about people's dresses, it seems so far."

"I don't even like *my* dress."

Casey thought her dress looked beautiful, but Jordan looked as if she was in physical pain just by virtue of wearing it. "Hopefully someone will get drunk and make a fool out of themselves—and it won't be a ZBZ or someone I've gone out with. Then there'll be something to talk about."

"We can only hope."

Through the thickening crowds of cocktail hour, with everyone racing to scarf down the best food and not look as though they were doing it, Casey relocated a somewhat exasperated Rob, who had her drink. "Cheers." They clinked glasses. "So…is this par for the course?" He didn't look as though he was used to the Greek social scene, especially the high-class version.

She sipped. "Sometimes there's a dramatic entrance or a weird couple that everyone immediately has to run off to a corner to judge, but so far it's been smooth sailing. Too smooth." She saw Ashleigh and Fisher approaching. "Hi."

"Hi!" Ashleigh was overexcited, as usual. "Oh—Fisher, this is Rob—Rob, Fisher." The men shook. "Rob works for Dean Bowman."

"How's that going for you?" Fisher asked.

"Pretty well. Tonight, the rich alums are clustered at the engineering gala," Rob said. "So the dean's happy. He has his priorities."

"Speaking of priorities," Ashleigh said, "Casey, behind you, it's Janette. Don't freak out."

"Janette? The Gamma Psi?"

"And the Panhellenic member who recommended I be expelled over the homecoming 'incident.'"

Casey did not freak out, or turn around. "Who's she talking to?"

"Katherine, her Gamma Psi sister and president of Panhellenic. This is totally the second board member I've seen her talking to tonight."

"Are they going to kick out the IKI girls?"

"I don't know if they have the power to do that. They're not bouncers. Not in those heels," Ashleigh said. "I don't know! Oh, she's coming this way. Act natural! Discuss!"

But they didn't have anything to discuss except the person coming their way, whom Ashleigh didn't properly identify and Casey couldn't turn her head to see without violating the rules of their "we're not spying" clause. The guys knew what to do—act oblivious—as they waited for the girl to reach them. "I can see that the ZBZ women are in order." *For now* was implied. It was Katherine, who was big on referring to sisters as "women" and not "girls." She looked at Rob. "I don't think we've formally met."

"I'm Rob Howell," he said, appropriately neutrally, adding, "I'm with Casey."

Score one for him, Casey decided.

Katherine nodded just as neutrally. "Moving on," she said, and left.

"Either something's in the water or she's up to something," Casey decided.

"She's not drinking water, and she's definitely up to something. I don't think she thinks much of ZBZ. Like she's waiting for us to screw up—as if we could possibly outshine the IKIs," Ashleigh said. "But can we not spend the night obsessing about Katherine? There's...Rebecca!" Ashleigh gestured to the ZBZ sister currently making her entrance. "With...Evan?" Because it did appear as though she had Evan Chambers on her arm. There was one hard glance in their direction, and then the couple headed into the crowd, going another way.

"Evan looks kinda coerced," Casey said, and she would know. She had dated him for almost three years. "That's... weird."

"You two are obsessed," Fisher said, and Casey turned to Rob, who notably hadn't said anything.

Instead he just said to Casey, "You're staring at me." It wasn't accusatory, but it could have been.

"Uh, so cat's out of the bag. Sort of." Ashleigh jumped in for Casey. A small mercy. "Rebecca mentioned in this extremely offhanded and super imprecise way that she knows you from somewhere."

"I interned in her father's office, for his chief of staff," he said without missing a beat. He didn't sound proud of it, but he wasn't hiding it, either. "Obviously, when he was still a senator, and not totally immersed in scandal. This was in high school. And before you say anything, I did not know anything about the whole prostitution ring thing. They don't tell interns about stuff like that. It was more like a congressional page program, but for senators. Less prestigious but a good résumé builder."

"So you kind of…crossed paths with Rebecca?" Casey prodded.

"Yeah." He nodded. "Look, it was a long time ago and not something I want to get into, okay?"

"In the past. Done," Casey said.

"Buried. Like, Valley of the Kings buried," Ashleigh said.

"You know they dug up the Valley of the Kings," Fisher said, more joking than to be unhelpful. Ashleigh gave him a little shove anyway. "Ow!" As if he was hurt by that.

Casey and Rob made the rounds, which for Casey meant greeting the rest of the Panhellenic board, all of whom were in attendance. One was more than eager to go on and on about university disciplinary councils—*way* too much information. But Casey struck gold with Lauren Parke, a slightly bubbly—meaning, inebriated—member whose term was expiring. She was more than happy to both bitch and praise the council and her tenure on it.

"Most of it is paperwork," Lauren said. "The university has its own codes of conduct for the Greek system, and there's a really long and boring but surprisingly complex binder. You could basically bring anyone up on anything if they don't know their rules. Fortunately most of the Greek presidents do. Weren't you president of ZBZ?"

"Interim."

"Right. That whole scandal. Anyway, we had to make a big deal out of it, but I think most of us were really just relieved it wasn't our houses that were subject to scrutiny. The university higher-ups and administration took care of most of the work. We were all sort of quiet. Suddenly we weren't the Panhellenic board—we were drunk, sex-crazed Greeks. So in a way we got off easy on the paperwork and telling off other members of the system. But most of the time, we're reciting rules to people who should already know them. The worst houses are the ones who are established, and on good terms with the university—you know, the boring ones—because they don't think they need to know the rules. The Inter-Fraternity Council seems far more interesting. The best house is Kappa Tau."

"Kappa Tau?"

"Oh, my God, they always have the best presidents when it comes to dodging the Greek system. Cappie is a master. He's quoted the rule book verbatim and pulled out some obscure thing to save Kappa Tau's butt more times than I can remember. He could probably find a way to join on IFC if he wanted to."

Casey snorted.

"The worst part is dealing with Nationals for different houses, when their senior officers call in wanting to know what's up with their houses. Because they have their own set of rules for behavior—and obviously the sororities are way stricter than the fraternities—and then the university has its rules, and I think at the end they don't want anyone to do anything but look pretty and have charity fundraisers. As if *they* didn't join a sorority to party."

"I've been to ZBZ Nationals," Casey said. She'd gone to the

ZBZ national convention the previous year. "There's a bit of self-delusion in the air. Or maybe ZBZ was all about feminine virtue sixty years ago."

Lauren laughed. "Totally. It was the same at Tri-Pi Nationals. Did they make you sing horrible songs?"

"And snap. ZBZ sisters don't clap. We snap."

"Oh, that's awesome. I know we used to be rivals, before Gamma Psi moved up in the ranks, but I think we all meld together in the end. After all, we attract the same type of pledges—girls who want to be sorority sisters." She shook her head. "This is my last term and I can't wait for some free time. Granted, it is a great résumé builder, and I'm glad I did it. I made a ton of contacts, but it's way too much work. I want to live a little before I work the rest of my life. Ooh, mini hot dogs. Do you know how many calories they have? Screw it, I can have one." She waved goodbye and went for the passing tray. "E-mail me if you have more questions!"

Casey retreated to a convenient balcony with Rob. "Sorry about that. Politics."

"I'm used to it. Just with less alcohol," he said. "I like it better with the alcohol."

She giggled. "I really didn't invite you so you could be subjected to the same things you're subjected to at work. There are good reasons to join the Greek system, by the way."

"Parties."

"Right. And not having to live in a dorm. And spring break. And a lot of stuff about being a big sister or little sister and a lifelong connection to a group of women who at times seem completely nuts. I think I made the best of the difficult parts. Actually it took a little getting used to, but there are definitely perks, once you get used to it. It can even be great.

The time of your life—except sometimes the social connections thing."

"Résumé building can be painful, but I think that's why it's called building," Rob said. "My résumé to get into college was full of things I built into it, and now my job résumé will be the same thing."

"Getting into Cyprus-Rhodes was the only reason I was vice president of my high-school literary magazine. I don't remember reading the submissions so much as arguing as long as possible as to which ones were the best. And they were all pretty terrible." That seemed so long ago, and so petty—was that how she would view college in four years? Or even less? "But hey, it got me into college."

"And Panhellenic will get you into grad school? Or just be a career builder?"

"There are some people with interesting jobs who are ZBZ sisters. And that *is* the reason a lot of people join sororities—because of their older, well-connected, job-offering sisters. I got a congressional internship because of a recommendation from Congresswoman Paula Baker over the summer. Again, great for the résumé."

"It does seem to always come down to that. Our lives down to a piece of paper."

"It's part of the reason I'm here—aside from you, of course. But before I met you, I was going, date or not. You were just…a happy accident." She wanted to reassure him, and he seemed to trust her on that. "I need contacts like Lauren if I'm going to get a term on Panhellenic next semester." Her phone rang. "Hold on. And I thought I shut this off. Hello?"

"Hey, Case. It's Betsy!"

Casey rolled her eyes at her overexuberant ZBZ sister, eager to prove herself. Way too eager. "Yes?"

"So this guy was here. He came to pick you up, but you weren't here."

"Rob already— Wait, what did he look like?"

"Um, hair was way too long, outfit kind of clashy? I don't mean hippie long, just a little too long. He's too short for that haircut."

"Was his name Dale?"

"He didn't give his name. He was really rushed. When I told him you left already he just ran off."

Crap! "Did he say where he was going?"

"Did he have to? Formal. Duh. But, no, he didn't."

"Great. Thanks." She cursed silently as she hung up. "Forget about it," she said, seeing Rob's inquisitive expression. "Where were we?"

"We were talking about why you came. Otherwise you would just sit at home? Or go to a much better party?"

"No! No, I was supposed to be at this engineering awards thing last night. I kind of promised my brother I would be his roommate's date. Dale's being honored for his grades and has this huge but totally innocent crush on me. But the awards event got moved to tonight."

"And?"

"And I had to choose, and I think the results are obvious. I told Dale by voice mail."

"How did he take it?"

"He showed up to pick me up anyway. Maybe. Betsy's a little oblivious, but I don't know any random guys who would be showing up to pick me up at the house."

Rob leaned against the railing. "He must be bummed."

"It was a pity date. Every link in this chain knew that. But maybe I should go—later, I mean."

"Later? It seems like you accomplished what you wanted here anyway."

"What?" She was taken back. "I'm here for you."

"And I appreciate it. It was a nice gesture, but it seems like a bad time for you. You're upset about breaking your promise."

"I'm not."

He shook his head. "I can see it in your face. And the fact that you've checked your cell phone like eight hundred times since I picked you up."

She unconsciously touched her purse, which contained her phone. "Maybe. But I would rather be with you. I want to be here with you."

He shrugged. "I'm around. I'm a student, and at night I have the social life of a transfer student—no friends because I wasn't here to network freshman year. A Greek formal is not the beginning and end of my social calendar."

"Are you bored? Is it that I'm boring you?"

"No." And he looked into her eyes when he said it. He wasn't evasive, as Evan or Cappie could be. "You're one of the most intelligent and interesting people I've met since my first day here. So…what I'm saying is I'm not going to drop off the earth at the end of the ball. I could even…I don't know, take you out another night? To something with less gossip and more fun?"

"Of course!" She jumped at the idea. "Yes! Yes, I would love to go out…to a movie or dinner or Dobbler's or something. Less formal. More social. More…date-y." She narrowed her eyes. "Why are you pushing me to go to the engineering event? Is it the stares Rebecca's giving you?"

"I like to think she's not staring. Is she?"

"Um, no," she lied, and he was probably smart enough to not believe her, but to accept her answer anyway.

"Look," he said, after glancing over his shoulder, "I've been involved in politics since I was twelve, and I know that if you're going to go into politics in any form, you're not going to get a lot of chances to do the right thing. And keeping your promise to a guy and not breaking his heart is doing the right thing."

He had a point. A solid, factual, gripping point. "You don't mind?"

He took her hand. "I'll escort you to your other date."

Casey had only one response to that. "You. Are. Amazing."

"I don't get that a lot. Maybe I should date girls who have other places to be more often." He laughed, and without further discussion, they left the formal together.

"Hey, have you seen Casey?" Dale half whispered to Rusty. "I went by her house and she was already gone."

Rusty could feel his palms clamming up. "She didn't call?"

"I dropped my phone in the sink again this morning. That thing is like, the least water-resistant technology I have ever encountered. I've had better experience with motherboards. A couple drops and it goes on the fritz. Once I answered it with a wet head from the shower—"

"Dale—"

"Anyway, no, she didn't call. No one's called me. Or I assume not."

"Dale." But he couldn't bring himself to say the words. This was Casey's responsibility, not his.

"Should I mention that? Cell phones and water? It is electrical engineering. It's a major issue. I've ruined three phones, two in the kitchen and one because my mom has this mystical ability to know when I'm just getting in or out of the shower. That seems like a good senior project—the water-resistant phone. The dean's here. I could propose it. You know, bounce it off him while he's relaxed, see how it goes. The senior project is a big deal and I'm a sophomore already. Or I could talk to the assistant dean. She seems nice. A little pale."

"Mercury poisoning. Dale—"

"Was I supposed to buy a corsage? You told me I wasn't supposed to. How am I supposed to impress Casey if I don't have the right things? I already don't have the right moves. Unless it's square dancing. Does your sister square-dance?"

"Dale, Casey is…over there." To his own shock, he saw his sister emerge from the hedges, dressed up for a formal but very present at this particular event. Upon spotting them, she came rushing up.

"Hi, Dale," she said. "Rus. Sorry I'm late. Sorority things."

While Dale stammered to greet his date, Rusty cut in, "Dale's phone broke this morning. So if you happened to send any messages, he *didn't get them*."

Casey got the message. "Oh, okay. Dale, sorry about your phone."

"I didn't break it. I dropped it and water destroyed it," Dale said, smiling nervously. "Hi, Casey. Thanks for coming."

She smiled back warmly. "I'm glad to be here."

chapter eight

Casey couldn't believe her luck. After playing both sides, she didn't deserve this. Her ill-crafted speech of apology to Dale for ditching him and then appearing late went up in smoke, thanks to Dale's inability to manage dishes and a cell phone at the same time, and Rusty had been there to tell her that before she started the embarrassing aforementioned speech, which would have been made only *more* embarrassing because of Dale's cluelessness. Of course, Dale spent the first five minutes in a stammering, sputtering daze, so with a nod to her brother, Casey sort of led him back into the event herself. Back in his element, Dale relaxed, regaling her with all the names of the important people he'd met, alumni and/or representatives of a prestigious graduate school or company on the hunt for new talent.

They were finishing off their cocktail hour on the green and moving into the reception area for the sit-down dinner, which was considerably less fancy and romantic than the Greek formal's setting but still classy. Only a few students were wearing jeans, and almost everyone had a jacket and tie. Aside from the speaker's podium, there were few decorations. The students outnumbered the alumni, but not by much, so no one was too swarmed.

Dale introduced her to a parade of deans, and though Casey was aware that he was unintentionally showing her off, she didn't mind it nearly as much as she'd imagined she might. They all regarded her with some respect—not as a sorority girl. She supposed they didn't know she was one, and Dale felt no need or compulsion to mention it. A couple of them asked her what her major was, and she said she was moving into political science, to which they responded positively again, though a few mentioned that the major was a little crowded, even if it was better than most liberal arts concentrations.

"I don't have a problem with liberal arts," said a Professor Girard, who was surprisingly young for a professor and apparently taught paleontology. "Have you done any internships?"

"Last summer." She listed the good parts of that internship, but not the bad.

"The real excitement is working for a campaign—but the pay can be spotty. It's about a real commitment to a cause," he said. "I volunteered on a campaign years ago for a mayor who might have gone to the White House, or so I stupidly said to him. A friend of mine who's far more cynical had a good laugh over it after the mayor's mistress overdosed in the hotel above campaign headquarters. And so I decided to focus on the politics of people who've been dead for at least two thousand years and leave their political commentary on tomb walls. But it is a good experience—and better if the candidate wins, of course."

"I heard working for a campaign might get you a job in the administration."

"It's not as guaranteed as you would think, but it's much better than trying to get a job with a losing candidate." He said he wouldn't be much help, but told her to take a certain class next semester if she could fit it into her schedule, and she thanked him.

"I didn't know you were so into politics," Dale said, having been silent through most of that conversation. He could really be polite when he wanted to be, which around her was pretty much all the time.

"What did you think I was into?"

He got flustered rather quickly, so much so that it was funny. "I, um…English literature?" Meaning, he had no idea what sorority girls did with their time, academically.

She just smiled at him, actually amused and seeing no reason not to show it, as he seemed to calm down when she smiled. "You don't have to answer. And I've been through a couple majors."

"It's good…to have a widespread…educational experience?" He was still searching for the right answer to impress her. She just tugged on his sleeve a little bit and they moved on.

When Casey finally read the program card on the table, she was shocked to recognize the name of the presenter of the award, not as a university person, but a big politico named a few times during her internship as being a go-to guy, especially for funding. Congresswoman Baker mentioned him once or twice in meetings or in passing. His name was Ted Griffin. Dale's reaction to hearing his name as a political figure was surprise. "I guess." He shrugged. "He is really rich. I think he invented some kind of electrical battery for airplane cockpits. Now he owns a controlling share in one of the airlines. Pretty cool for an engineer. Also I heard he skydives. Like Richard Branson."

"Are we going to meet him?"

"Yeah, sure. I guess so." He wasn't nearly as enthused, but he was Dale, the engineer, and this night was about him, not politics. Still, Casey saw no reason not to try to snatch an opportunity to talk to Griffin, who might have interesting advice—or at least remember her name and face in the future when she introduced herself in some other situation. "Maybe there'll be time, you know, after the ceremony. Oh, hey, Cappie. You made it."

At which point, Casey's sky significantly darkened. Which for nighttime was saying something. Her heart leaped into her throat. She tried to swallow it down, but it wouldn't stop pounding.

There was Cappie in all his glory—with a suave dark suit and his hair halfway combed but still adorably tousled. "Hey, Dale." Completely casually, he exchanged a respect-knuckle complicated handshake with Dale. "Casey." It was remarkable with how little emotion he said it, at least in front of Dale. "What are you doing here?"

"What are *you* doing here?"

"Uh, I have a wide spectrum of social activities and interests. Such as seeing my buddy Daley here get honored. Also, Casey, I'm dating your brother."

"He's Rusty's plus-one since Jordan's at the formal," Dale explained, completely oblivious to her panic. "He has someone sitting in for him for the formal."

"And I assume Heath will carry out his presidential duties with all of the dignity the office requires," Cappie said. "Did you know Dean Kessin knows how to hot-wire a car?"

"I totally did not know that," Dale said. "That's awesome. For, like, emergencies of course."

"It seems like tonight is just full of surprises," Casey said through her teeth.

After Dale ran off to freshen his drink, Casey closed in on Cappie so they wouldn't be overheard. "Are you stalking me?"

"*Stalking* is a word I've been hearing a lot lately. And with all due respect to the actual word, I must admit that hearing about your attendance as Dale's date was a somewhat persuasive argument in my social decisions. Also, the All-Greek Formal sucks and everyone knows it."

"But you've never missed it."

"Fine. If it makes you feel better, Rebecca was stalking me—to use the popular term—via text message all day today, asking me to be her date."

"You broke up with Rebecca…when?"

"Way, way too long ago to go down that road again. Not when she's so desperate. What's up?"

Casey sighed. "Long story. Actually, a long story that doesn't really have an ending. She's obsessed with avoiding this transfer student she knows from high school."

"Juicy."

"Neither of them will admit to the thing that keeps them apart like—"

"Opposite ends of magnetic poles?"

She stared at him.

"Sorry, I think it's in the water here. And I was an engineering major—"

"For two days."

"You either have an excellent memory, or you're hyperfocused on my personal history. I wonder which one it is. Or which is more stalker-ish."

"Don't embarrass me."

"In front of whom? The dean of engineering? Your brother? Because one of those you don't know and couldn't care less about, and the other has already seen me embarrass you at least half a dozen times. Seven to be precise."

"Just…don't? Okay?"

Cappie seemed to grasp the severity of her tone, and the situation—for once. "Fine. Best behavior."

"So, why are you really here?"

"Open bar. There, that's the final lousy excuse I'm giving." He half smiled at her and walked off.

Finding herself flustered for some reason, Casey actually welcomed the return of Dale with another drink for her, even if it was soda. "So," he said, "did you see the ice sculpture?"

"No," Casey said, "but I would love to." Because if he didn't put his tongue on it first, Cappie could get involved in a conversation with the ice sculpture.

Jordan's night could be going better. Admittedly no disasters had occurred. Her heels hadn't broken, because she was wearing flats; Rusty hadn't recently had a major crisis she had to talk him through; and no one from ZBZ had done anything truly embarrassing yet. She finally stopped texting Rusty long enough to look around for Casey, but couldn't find her. She did find Ashleigh and Fisher, a couple she loved, and the fact that they weren't accepted as a couple because he was a hasher just stood as another example of the ridiculously obnoxious Greek system. So Ashleigh was dating the kitchen guy. She wasn't above him. This wasn't the nineteenth century.

"Have you seen Casey?"

"Oh, she left," Ashleigh said. "I know! *Shocker.* And it wasn't because of the formal, or so she said in a message on my phone. She went to the engineering event. Rob even took her. Not sure how that works out, her having two dates at once, but she's managing."

"Oh." It seemed that Casey was smarter than she was and had found an excuse to leave.

"I'm sure Rusty would have come if he could have," Ashleigh said, slightly misinterpreting her plight. "And at least he didn't drag you to the engineering event and make you miss the formal."

"It was very nice of him," Jordan said, because it was the only possible answer that was appropriate. In a depressed haze she returned to the bar. "I hate these things."

"Oh, my God! How can you say that?" said the girl next to her, who couldn't have been more than a junior, if that. "Open bar. I mean you need an ID, but I have one. Do you need a drink?"

She looked at the overly dressed—even for a formal—fellow student and said, "No, thanks."

The other girl finished her drink. "Okay, if not for the bar, this thing would be totally boring. I'm supposed to have guys falling to the floor over me, and that is totally not happening."

"I didn't know that was supposed to happen."

"What, that wasn't promised to you when you were introduced to the sororities? Are you someone's date?"

"I'm a ZBZ," Jordan answered, surprised at her own indignation and need to defend her house. Maybe she *was* a ZBZ.

"Oh, my God! You are what I should totally be. I don't know you, and I had to memorize everything about everybody. You're a pledge?"

Jordan nodded. "Jordan."

"Linda. I was a ZBZ last year, but—and don't get all judgmental—I left with Frannie to join IKI."

"I don't judge." She did, but in this case, what she said was true. Sometimes the sororities were hard to tell apart anyway. "Why did you leave, if I can ask?"

"Um, politics. You know the story?"

"I've heard it told a couple different ways, but never the IKI way."

Linda swallowed the cherry from her drink. "ZBZ last year was a mess. When I accepted my offer, they were the most distinguished house with the best, nicest, prettiest girls on campus and Frannie was the most awesome president ever. I was thrilled. Then there was that whole scandal with Jen K., my pledge sister. I ran a marathon for charity with her! She was kinda weird, but she was a legacy so they had to let her in, and they didn't suspect anything until she wrote the article about ZBZ and Greek life in general. From there everything was terrible—for everyone, but especially for ZBZ. Nationals sent this crazy woman to tell us how to act and instituted all kinds of crazy traditions and then Casey actually *kept* some of them when she left. ZBZ was not a fun place.

"Frannie told us to lie to the woman from Nationals, so we did, then Casey went behind her back and told the truth, and we all looked like liars. So Casey was made interim president, but Frannie came back, staying a fifth year and running for president *again,* even though she'd been president and was kicked out for her presidential decisions. So she ran a really mean campaign, and Casey ran a mean campaign right back and we all knew things we didn't want to know about either of them, and Rebecca was like, 'choose a side.' And we all decided to take *her* side, because she was so organized and thoughtful, and we voted in Ashleigh. And that was another disaster, because she wasn't running and totally did not want to be president and was much worse than Casey or Frannie and totally needed Casey's help to do anything at first."

Jordan just nodded.

"So all through Hell Week, I'm thinking I've spent a year of college memorizing handbooks and cheers and snapping instead of clapping and looking beautiful all the time and doing demeaning pledge chores, and for what? To listen to a bunch of older students bicker like they're in high school? I couldn't take it anymore, but if I walked out, I would never be in a sorority. So Frannie offered me a fresh start with this new house she was founding, and I hadn't been personally involved with anything bad Frannie did, and it was really my only option, so I said yes." She looked out at the bar, at nothing in particular. "I guess I shouldn't be so judgmental because I wasn't thinking critically, as Frannie made all these promises to get us to leave and she didn't deliver on most of them and I should have expected that after all I'd been through in the past year, but I still had trust. Uh, this is just between us, right?"

Instead of swearing to it, Jordan shrugged her shoulders. "I don't have anyone else to tell."

"Okay, because I shouldn't be going on like this, but you get it, right? I had no choice. Sort of. I had two choices, and one of them was bad and one of them was sounding better."

"I don't get the whole system anyway, so, yeah, I can understand that."

"So we get to school and move into this house and it's a mess because Frannie couldn't afford a house hasher, and now the pledges refuse to do anything because they know that we've been dissolved and they have no reason to invest any time in IKI. Not that I blame them. They're smarter than us, I can tell you that. And we have a creepy psycho landlady who's always drunk and touchy. The only reason we're still living there is we have nowhere else to go. All the dorms are filled up and it was too late to find other housing." Linda looked depressed—or suicidal, just from her expression. "I miss what it all used to be like at ZBZ before this whole mess. We had a lot of fun times. But after everything that's happened, I don't know if anyone there would accept me back."

"I would be okay with that."

There was a sparkle of hope in Linda's eyes. "Really?"

"Sure. You've already said you left for reasons that were important at the time but you were misled. If you pledged ZBZ, spent a year in ZBZ as a pledge, and then abandoned it because people were doing stupid political things, I wouldn't hold it against you."

"Really? You are so awesome. What's your name again?"

"Jordan. But I'm just a pledge."

"You're an awesome pledge. Do us all a favor and don't depledge."

Jordan smiled for the first time that evening. "I'll do my best."

Cappie made good on his word—for the moment, at least—and Casey didn't see much of him. Despite looking, against her better judgment. After the initial rounds, Dale got caught up talking to some alumni about something technical, and Casey was on her own. She took a seat and removed her shawl and took the opportunity to get off her feet for a moment. It would be a serious faux pas to remove her heels at an event, even an engineering honors ceremony, but it was good to not be standing directly on them for a few minutes.

She had to admit, though, the event was pleasant. Maybe this evening wasn't the disaster she'd made it out to be in her panicked rush a few minutes earlier. Maybe it wouldn't be so bad after all.

She lifted her head at the squeal of the microphone being adjusted. The awards ceremony had started. Before they got to the current students' awards, they had a few honors to graduate students, and she was about to tune out when she heard Max's name called out. Her heart seemed to leap into her throat as she craned her head to see him, but he wasn't there. Of course, he was in England. His faculty advisor came to retrieve his award on his behalf in his absence. She gave a short speech about Max, only a few lines, about how dedicated he was to the things he cared about. Suddenly cold without her sash, Casey shivered and held her arms, her pulse rising, until she noticed someone looking at her. Not staring—just looking, rather politely, with concern. It was not her brother or her date, but Cappie. Max would love to be here, his faculty advisor said, but he had obligations in England. What she didn't know was, he had no obligations here—no girl to tie him down. In fact his overseas move might even have been inspired by one particular girl, a senior and sorority girl, who'd chosen a guy who refused to commit to her over Max. That guy was Cappie, and unlike Max, he was here.

She'd lost Max but suddenly she didn't feel so lost.

chapter nine

"Wow. Engineering social—not so bad," Ashleigh said, looking up from her phone and the text message from Casey. "Who knew?"

Fisher, up for anything as usual, only shrugged. "People surprise you. Even engineers. I used to go out with one."

"There are female engineers?"

"A strange genetic aberration, I know. No, it's more common than you think. Just not common enough for the *male* engineers. They had no chance with her. If she'd made a signal that they did, it would have been a feeding frenzy. The hazards of a program with an uneven gender ratio."

"Like English lit. But other way around."

"There are totally guys in English lit."

"Yeah, but mainly girls. Most guys are fulfilling their core requirements or are *way* too into English literature."

"Any other majors we should make huge generalizations about?"

"Not off the top of my head." She waved to the approaching couple. "Rebecca. Evan Chambers."

"I come without my last name, you know," Evan said, not truly annoyed, but definitely not thrilled either. As to Rebecca hanging on his arm, he was surprisingly neutral. In fact, one could say he was even having a good time. "Actually, right now I think I'm more an Evan than a Chambers."

"Welcome to the world of the dispossessed," Fisher said, and they bumped knuckles. "Me? I wash dishes at a sorority, but it's not nearly as bad as you would think. I kind of lucked out, actually." His other arm squeezed his girlfriend's. "The job's full of opportunities."

"Life is full of surprises," Rebecca said. She was rather conspicuously looking around.

Ashleigh jumped in for her. "Casey and Rob left."

"They did?"

"Casey decided to go to the engineering event. Promises or something."

"Oh. So she dumped him?"

"No, they'd just both had enough of the formal."

"Oh."

Fisher looked at Evan during this conversation, and he just shrugged, but didn't detach from Rebecca or run away from his current obligation. The news didn't affect him at all, even if Rebecca visibly relaxed.

"Since everyone else has already asked already, maybe I should give it a shot," Fisher said. "Hey, Rebecca, what's the deal with this Rob guy?"

"I need a drink," Rebecca announced, and instead of asking Evan to get one, which would have been entirely appropriate for the formal setting, she spun around on her heels and left for the bar.

Evan was the first to speak. "Ouch."

"I had it coming," Fisher said.

"So…are you going out with Rebecca?"

Evan just shrugged. "She asked me to escort her to the formal. I was stag. I said yes. That's the whole story. Not very interesting."

"Did she mention why?"

"Probably." But he was not being helpful, and left to join his date.

Ashleigh crossed her arms. "Definitely a conspiracy."

"Or he's just doing the stand-up thing. And he was dateless," Fisher suggested. "He probably doesn't know any more than we do. Why would she tell him?"

"I don't know. She's Rebecca. Woman of mysterious and cold calculations."

"Hey, I thought you were supposed to be listening in on the gossip on other houses, not ZBZ. Can't you do that enough at the house, keeping track of the pledges?"

"Really the talk is mostly about IKI, because this party is lame and nothing else interesting has happened." In the corner of her eye she could see Rebecca talking to a dean. "I need spy equipment. Like headphones and microphones in the plants. Ooh, and a teeny-tiny camera in a corsage or something."

"I bet someone at the engineering bash could make you one of those."

"That thing is sounding better all the time. But at least the dancing is starting. Want to?"

"Nothing could make me happier," Fisher said. A slight exaggeration on his part, but definitely better than standing around. It was a better use of his feet. They moved to the now-open dance floor, where couples were assembling. "See, this is why Evan said yes."

"Because he likes to dance? Do you know something I don't?"

"Because being single at this exact moment would suck," he said, squeezing her hands. "And I'm glad I'm not."

"Do you want to dance?"

Jordan looked up from her phone and saw Calvin standing in front of her, having swept in when she was not paying attention to her surroundings. "Are you serious?"

"About as serious as you need me to be," he said. "Look, you're a ZBZ, and I'm an Omegi Chi. It's my manly duty to ask a lady to dance. But if you don't want to, I totally understand."

"Do you like dancing?"

He shrugged. "To be honest, it's not really my type of atmosphere."

"And to be honest," Jordan said with a smile, "my feet are killing me. I don't think I could dance if I both knew how *and* wanted to. Neither of which is true."

"Then can I escort a lady to a seat?"

Jordan offered her hand. "I would be thrilled."

He took her hand and, with all the formality of their surroundings, escorted her to a seat at one of the tables around the dance floor, where they both promptly collapsed.

"I don't have as much to complain about, I know," Calvin said, "but I think my feet spread over the summer. My shoes are killing me."

"My heart bleeds for you."

He looked at the phone in her hands. "How's Rusty?"

"Typing way too fast. So he's either overeager to talk or he's busy. Probably both."

"Anyone die of food poisoning yet?"

"You heard about that? He says that was totally not his fault. And I think he's right. *He* didn't undercook the food. Either way, his event still sounds way better than this. I'm supposed to be supporting my sisters, but all they want to do is gossip and it gets old."

"I know the feeling," Calvin said. "Even though guys aren't supposed to gossip, we totally do. Or just try to look interested in everyone else."

She put a hand on his shoulder. "You have it tough, I have to admit."

"Hey, I get to look good in a tux, the food is good and the bill's on Panhellenic. I'm not exactly suffering, at least above my knees." He looked out at the seemingly happy crowd, and back at Jordan. "So—do you want to dance?"

"Do you think Rusty will feel threatened?" she said jokingly.

"Rusty is the first person I came out to at Cyprus-Rhodes and the least likely to feel threatened. And it'll kill some time before the main course." He offered his hand. "My lady?"

She smiled and, against her best instincts, took his hand. "I've changed my mind. I would love to dance."

Casey made a conscious effort to stop deciding if her night was going well or not. Things had changed course too many times for her to keep track. She decided to live in the moment, and the moment seemed to come when she was getting up from her table to find and check on her brother and a crowd of people passed by, followed by a man in a ridiculously stylish but still sort of offbeat suit—and it wasn't Cappie. Even Casey recognized Ted Griffin, though he looked shorter in person, and the little bits of gray were more evident in his beard than when he appeared in magazines.

"Hello," he said. "I think I'm supposed to congratulate you now."

"Oh! I'm not an engineer. My engineer is…off, somewhere. He's Dale. Dale Kettlewell. I'm Casey Cartwright."

He didn't rush off, or even excuse himself. He nodded. "What's your major? If you've declared."

"Political science."

"I would have thought more about minoring in that, if I knew how political being a public figure could be back when I was in college," he said. "Sorry, Ted Griffin."

"I know. I mean, I've heard about you. And read about you." Fortunately she was not a gushing fan, but she did feel a little flustered anyway. "I'm sure Cyprus-Rhodes is honored by your presence."

"They were less honored when I was a student," he replied. "And I didn't have a 4.0 grade point average every semester. It's hard to do that and have a social life, and I was a Kappa Tau, so that cut into a lot of study time."

"It is a difficult balance. Wait, you were a KT?"

Griffin smiled. "I'd do the secret handshake but you don't look like a KT. Unless things have really changed around here."

"No, no. The KTs are…pretty much the slacker party house. No offense."

"None taken."

Think, Casey, think! Say something smart! And intriguing. "I read your critique of laptop batteries." It was the only thing she could think of that he'd written that she'd actually read, by chance, while surfing the Internet when she was looking him up during her internship. Suddenly she realized she couldn't make much of a conversation about it beyond its title.

"It was a very intriguing article," Cappie cut in, to her distress. She glared at him, but he focused on Mr. Griffin. "*Newsweek,* right? I agree—and so does Casey, sorry, she's a friend of mine—that battery technology is way behind computer and phone technology. My laptop dies in two hours."

"Are you running nonessential programs?"

"Just Microsoft Word. It's really a problem. But—not being, I confess, an engineer myself, I don't fully understand the problems of electrical engineering in batteries. We're a simple folk, we liberal arts people."

Griffin laughed. "I took the history of literary criticism and I didn't find it so simple, just more conclusive than my article, which was mostly to complain about the state of things. *Newsweek* likes that."

"They are big on critical articles," Casey said, not sure if she was cutting in on Cappie or supporting him. But she did, fortunately, know the nontechnical areas of *Newsweek* very well, or had read up on them since trying to switch her major. "I can't tell if they're legitimately trying to start a national conversation or just going against the grain for attention."

"Going against conventional wisdom is always good for attention, and attention is always good for readership," Griffin said. "I like to think they're a bit more altruistic than that, but that's the engineer in me talking and not the politician. Which, somewhat sadly, I am often categorized as because I get behind causes. Of course it's not all bad—there are plenty of good reasons to go into politics."

"Or at least understand them," Cappie said. "Me, I'm just a women's studies major—currently—but Casey here is the expert."

She blushed. "I wouldn't say that." Was she actually happy that he was praising her, or still too cynical? She didn't have time to decide. "I am very interested in a career in politics—the nobler side, if it exists."

"Questioning its existence is showing more sense than most starry-eyed youngsters." Griffin laughed. "Did I just say 'starry-eyed youngsters'? I must be getting old. Well, I did take the long route, making the money first, though that wasn't my intention when I started working in airplane development. Life can be pleasantly surprising."

"You did revolutionize how airline cockpits are designed," Cappie baited.

He waved it away. "Like anyone's interested in that. Okay, maybe the electrical engineers—but they have to do better, not the same. They discuss it with dollar signs in their eyes sometimes, like mechanical devices all come with a huge payout. That's only slots and only if you hack one."

"You hacked a slot machine?" Cappie said, with too much interest, probably.

Griffin's face lit up. "It was supposed to be my senior project, but the deans shot it down. I built a device that sent electrical signals to confuse the magnets in the machine—and this was before it was all done with microchips. Now I think it would be even easier. I never got to test it in an actual casino, but I did get it working on a kiddy slot that paid out tokens on a boardwalk. The deans were not interested in magnifying this accomplishment by recognizing it."

"That does sound like the deans," Casey said. "Ours are pretty much the same."

"It's strange what life does to you. I thought all deans came from some dark, angry place when I was in college. And now I'm here, and the Bowster is the dean."

"Dean Bowman was the Bowster? That was his name?" Cappie snickered.

Ted Griffin lowered his voice. "If you use it, you didn't get it from me. Wait a few weeks so it's less obvious, okay? I'd like to stay on speaking terms with him. And, no, I can't spend the night telling Bowster stories, much as I'd like to. I think everyone would appreciate it far more than me going on about the accomplishment of a 4.0 grade point average—even the people *with* 4.0 grade point averages." He had a mischievous twinkle in his eye. "I do respond to e-mails. Why don't you take my card—what's your name, young man? There I go again! Young man!"

"Cappie," he said, as Griffin produced business cards from the breast pocket of his jacket.

Griffin gave him one, and then said, "Casey Cartwright, right?"

She smiled and accepted the card. "Yes."

"I was always good with names. Not actually talking to women, but getting their names right. I had that going for me, but not a lot else. It's good to talk to someone who knows more than their way around the wiring of a black box. Shoot me an e-mail sometime if you have a question you think I can answer—and not just whether to cut the red wire or the green wire."

"Thank you very much."

He smiled and left them, to be rather suddenly jumped by another horde of admirers and deans, and Casey looked at the card in disbelief. "What was that about?"

"Chatting it up with Ted Griffin? Pretty basic concept, actually," Cappie said.

She put the card in her pocketbook. "I don't know why you did what you just did—if you did something intentionally, just because he was a KT—"

"He was a KT? Seriously? *Awesome.*"

Casey rolled her eyes, but at least Cappie hadn't known.

"Anyway," Cappie said, "as to doing something intentionally, I refuse to answer that question. I prefer to remain a man of mystery."

"Thank you. I think."

He bowed. "My lady." And, as promised, he disappeared again, but this time she wasn't as thrilled with his departure as before. He wasn't being embarrassing, he was just being Cappie. The good part of Cappie, the one she liked.

"You know, you're not obligated to do this."

Evan slowly moved in a circular motion, so that Rebecca would spin around to the beat of the slow dance. He wasn't the most coordinated person, but he knew how to dance whatever dance was required of him at a Greek formal.

"I thought you wanted to. Unless *you* don't want to dance."

Which he would think odd, because she'd accepted his invitation somewhat eagerly. "I mean stay with me," Rebecca said, with a hard edge to her voice, but the menace didn't seem directed at him. "The premise of this date was for you to serve as a buffer between me and Rob. He's gone. You're free to do as you please."

"I like to think of myself as more than a buffer."

"I'm serious."

"And I'm serious. You asked for a date, you have one. Unless you want me to ditch you for some reason. Am I that repulsive?"

Rebecca softened her expression, which, Evan noticed, she wore very well. "No. I just thought I should let you know I'm relieving you of any perceived obligation."

"Then call this one a freebie," he said. "Also, if you haven't noticed, I'm obligated to be here, and somewhat dateless myself, having driven away everyone important in my life."

"Frannie was important?"

He shivered. "Frannie was…Frannie. She could make herself important. And she was, for what it's worth, my girlfriend for a time. It counts for something. The motivation behind it wasn't good on her side…but I wasn't a saint, either."

"You're cutting her a lot of slack."

"I have a newfound sympathy for people in bad positions and trying to make the best of it," he said. He hadn't loved Frannie, but he wouldn't dismiss her so easily, as all of her former ZBZ sisters were eager to do. "Frannie and I are over. What she does from here isn't my business at the moment, and hopefully won't be my business in the future—if I have a business."

Rebecca actually sounded supportive. "You still have law school."

"It remains to be seen whether I need a scholarship or they'll take my car instead of tuition."

"Why did you throw away your trust fund?"

"It was more that I told my parents off—"

"Something I can relate to—"

"—and they're the keys to my trust fund. Somewhat literally. It started getting crazy. At first there was this whole list of decisions about my life made by them that I had to follow to keep it. Then they decided to take away my money anyway because I said something that implied that I didn't know what to do with it. As if any college kid knows what to do with millions of dollars." He could actually say a number around Rebecca, who was not without her own fortune, somewhat mitigated by circumstances surrounding her father's failing political career. "It got to be too much. Their rules kept changing, so I decided I didn't want to play by them anymore. So it's life on the open road."

"Whatever you do, don't go to Alaska."

"Why?"

"You didn't see that movie about that kid who gave all his money to charity and hitchhiked across the country, only to die of starvation in Alaska because he forgot to buy a map? I forget the name. Sean Penn directed it."

"Into the Wild."

"Right. That. Don't go to Alaska."

"And forget to buy a map and starve to death."

"Yes."

He laughed. "That's not on my agenda, but I'll take it into consideration."

"I don't see you as a wild-eyed hippie nature freak anyway."

"Really? What gave you that impression? My filthy-rich lifestyle?"

"You're an Omega Chi."

"You know, I wasn't always," he said. "I pledged Kappa Tau first."

"They didn't take you?"

"They were a little too ambivalent for my tastes. I suppose if Egyptian Joe had been any more enthusiastic about me, I would be at their party right now, with a plastic beer can hat over my head and that horrible goatee I had freshman year."

Now Rebecca smiled at the image. "Or you would be president, and you would be here."

"In some alternate universe, maybe."

"You don't sound like you regret it."

He shrugged. "I know it's like my ritual duty to be down on the Kappa Taus, but really, they just weren't the right fit for me. For Cappie, they're perfect. Omega Chi is just my place—one of the few things I've ever been sure of in my life, on my own, that was not an idea introduced by my parents. They didn't tell me to pledge, even if it would be good for my career. They didn't say anything about it. I went from Kappa Tau to Omega Chi and I don't think they even noticed until I had some officer position. It was all my decision." Realizing they'd been talking about him for too long, he said, "Did your parents tell you not to pledge?"

"They told me not to make a fool of myself, so I did. The fact that I did it while wearing a ZBZ T-shirt and being filmed by drunken guys at spring break was just incidental and more of a hassle in the end. But it was worth it, however much crap I had to put up with when I got back to the house and Nationals complained about my behavior. It was my choice. What I wanted to do at that exact moment and no one could tell me differently, even though some people tried."

"Casey?"

"And Cappie."

"Rebecca, if Cappie's telling you not to do something, then you probably shouldn't do it. Or you should because it's just that wild. It's some kind of seal of approval for wildness."

"I suppose."

"I don't know. I'm too tired of judging people. Do whatever you want. Whatever makes you happy."

"I can't tell if being destitute has made you wise or crazy."

Evan said, "Neither can I."

chapter ten

Rusty Cartwright felt that, for the first time in weeks, there was no reason to panic. The engineering event was going well. Everyone was here for the most part. No one was ill, and Professor Boyden's faint proved just a dramatic flourish in front of the alumni from Microsoft. Raul Gonzalez didn't have a high position in the company, but that didn't stop him from being mobbed by every disgruntled professor and overeager student looking for the name of a director of human resources and possibly a word of recommendation. But Rusty had two years before he had to worry about that.

"Good job, Mr. Cartwright," his advisor, Hastings, said to him as people were seated for the actual awards ceremony. "Get your grades back up and you might just be getting a trophy next year." He turned his back on Rusty and was gone just as quickly as he appeared.

"Thank you," he said.

"He's a dick," Cappie added.

"Yeah."

"Spitter, if you want a trophy, just find a trophy store and buy one."

"I know where it is. That's how I got these." He gestured to the tacky track trophies lined up in rows by the podium.

"That's how Kappa Tau got all of our trophies."

"You mean the ones that weren't stolen."

"That was implied. Also, Beaver added his soccer participation trophies from elementary school last year to make things a little more crowded."

"You get those awards just for showing up."

"Ask him how he got that scar on his hand."

"You can't play soccer with your hands. It's, like, the *one* rule."

"And that's what makes it a great story."

Rusty shook his head. The deans were taking their places on the dais, preparing for Griffin's speech and the awards ceremony itself, brief though it was. "Did you just come here to stalk my sister?"

"Again with that word. *Stalk*. It's so harsh."

"Answer the question."

"Please. The free food and open bar were also great motivators."

"You could have gotten those at the formal that I had to miss to make sure the courses were served in the correct order."

"Formals are lame. Always have been, always will be. Provided no one gets drunk and does something embarrassing—all the more likely with my presence elsewhere—there's nothing about it that's memorable."

"Maybe if your girlfriend was there…"

"Is that what this is about? You have a phone. Call her and invite her to this shindig. Or at least the after-party."

"I can't ask Jordan to miss the Greek event of the semester."

Casey looked at his watch. "It's half over. She's a girl, so her feet are killing her, her hair has the consistency of a brush tree and she just realized it by trying to straighten it in the mirror. You're doing her a favor."

"She's supposed to support her sisters."

"Unless one of them is in a wheelchair and she's on push duty, she's not supporting anything. Trust me on this one."

It was appealing. "I'll call her."

"Good man." Cappie slapped him on the back and disappeared in the direction of the bar.

Rusty sighed and watched the deans haphazardly try to find the correct seats. The microphone worked—he'd tested it. And at this point, he really didn't care. He'd had very little sleep over the past few days, and it was starting to get to him. Even if Cappie was right about the formal, Rusty still wanted to be there and find out for himself. With Jordan. No way could dancing with her be lame.

"Why so glum, chum?" It was Chris McFadyen, the polymer scientist who worked in Silicon Valley. He wasn't that much older than Rusty—ten years at most. "Wow. I can't believe I just said that. Anyway, job well done, if you were organizing this thing. Weren't you?"

"I helped out." He didn't mention his connection to the now-infamous Thursday-night caterers. "I got roped into it by Professor Hastings, actually. I skipped out of a study session with him to go to a party, and he was pissed. So I'm making it up to him."

"Flattery will only get you so far," Chris said. "I remember him. I had him freshman year and again as a senior. Hated his class both times. But I got through them."

"With a 4.0 grade point average? Because I started okay, but mine's been slipping."

"I know two things—one, that I didn't get a tacky trophy for any grade point average, and two, that I didn't go to enough parties. So really, the worst of both worlds." Chris rubbed his goatee. He did look sort of like a hippie, if in a formal suit, because it was with sandals. "In college everything seems like a big deal, and when you get out, it's really not. The things you worried about seem worthless and the good moments seem better. But the professors don't tell you that college isn't the center of the universe because otherwise you might take them less seriously. I can't blame them—college is the center of *their* universe. Every year a crowd leaves and a fresh crowd appears for them to impress and remold in their image, knowing that these students will forget their names by the end of next semester, if they bothered to learn them at all."

"That makes it sound depressing," Rusty admitted. Maybe he shouldn't have, but he did.

"Some of them might think that. And some of them might legitimately just care about the joy of teaching. Or maybe some of them couldn't find jobs in the real world, and make themselves up to be tyrants in their own worlds here. Not that people don't get megalomaniac in the private sector, either. Or the public sector. The short story is, people are jerks because they need to feel important. But they're only as important as you let them be. Sometimes it's wise to suck up, sometimes you just ignore them, hand in your papers and move on. I can tell you that a 3.5 is not a whole lot different from a 4.0 to a corporation, except the latter implies you might not have had a social life and developed the skills you need to talk your way into that giant company you want to hire you. And then you can go on to be a salaried employee, slowly making your way up the ladder until college calls and gives you a free room at the local hotel if you'll hang out with current students with a few shots of scotch in you."

Rusty smiled. "How's life after college?"

"Drinks cost more. It's ridiculous, really. Take advantage of the opportunities you have now. Free beer! Ha, I love it." He slapped him hard on the back. "You have my card, right?"

"Right. Thank you, Mr. McFadyen."

"Chris! My name is Chris." And, a little drunk, he shambled off, leaving Rusty to digest his rambling and dubious wisdom.

Rusty opened his phone, then remembered he had used up his invitation. Did it really matter this late in the night? He called Jordan. "Hey. Want to crash an engineering bash? And by that I mean, act politely and eat their desserts."

"Yes. Any reason to get out of here," Jordan said.

"You might have some trouble at the door."

"Do you know any engineers who are stag?"

Rusty looked around the room at his fellow classmates chatting it up with the alumni. There was a serious disparity in the numbers between men and women. "Do you even have to ask?"

"I'm gone," Jordan said to Calvin on her way out. "Don't tell the other pledges I'm ditching."

"Why would I? And where are you going?"

"The engineering event. Rusty got me an invite through his lab partner."

Calvin shook his head. "Anywhere but here?"

"I hope they don't have a dress code that involves heels," she said. "Wait, they're engineers."

"Exactly."

Jordan waved to Calvin with more exuberance than she'd shown the entire evening and ran off, barefoot, into the night and on to better things. Calvin straightened his cummerbund and returned to the dance hall.

"Why the long face?"

Calvin, mystified, looked at Heath.

"Yeah, I know, lame question. I've got another one with a frown and Charlie Brown. But seriously."

"Everyone has pretty much left the formal or didn't come. Or is dancing with their ex for some reason, if she could even be considered that." He was looking at Evan and Rebecca, who by all appearances were actually enjoying themselves. "Or at least they have someone to dance with."

"I thought you were going out with Michael, the TA?"

"No, so over that. He scared me off with his Moroccan food."

"It was that bad?"

He chuckled. "No, it was just…too much. Like, he would probably say I should have brought him to the dance. That I should be proud and not afraid to make waves."

Heath nodded. "It would be wicked awkward. I wouldn't do it, although the Kappa Taus who actually came are too wasted to care."

"Yeah, aren't you acting president or something?"

"Cappie wanted to go to the honors engineering awards, for some reason. He picked my name out of the goldfish bowl. I should really abuse my powers and do something interesting and tyrannical, but it seems like too much effort. Clearly I have all the makings of great leadership." Heath studied him. "You would be a good president. Of Omegi Chi anyway. You have…authority. A sense of responsibility. You're not wasted after lunch every day."

"Look, it was hard enough for me during pledge year. You think I would win an election? First gay president of Omegi Chi?"

"Dude, you're gonna end up being a lot of 'first gay' things in your life. Just...embrace it."

"Now you sound like Michael."

"Ouch. Okay, sorry. Still smarting from that?"

"I'm over Michael," Calvin said. "Just not...other people." His eyes went in search of his roommate, Grant, as if he would find him, but Grant wasn't here. "People I can't be seen with in public."

"Sounds complicated."

"Dating in the house. Bad idea. Even if it seems...really great."

"In the *Omega Chi* house?"

"Yeah, you know Grant? And, uh, don't tell anybody?"

Heath nodded knowingly. "I know how to keep a secret." He was clearly trying to be helpful. "I heard that's a problem at coed fraternities. They have to watch out for pledges who are just trying to get in to get with someone in the house."

Cyprus-Rhodes had no coed fraternities, so Calvin could only guess at the consequences of such a situation. "It would make pledging even more complicated. And it is pretty complicated as it is." He looked around the room again. "Totally should have gone to the engineering event. I wasn't invited, but I could have managed."

"You are smooth. Why are you here?"

"Because I like looking good in a tux."

Health smiled. "You do look good in a tux."

"Thank you. And Evan looks good in a tux. I say that because he should, because I almost had to freakin' dress him to get him here. Little brother responsibilities do not go away after pledge year."

Heath may not have known the whole story with Evan, but he did know enough to say, "Is he going out with Rebecca?"

"No, I don't think so. She came up to him right before the formal—like, as we were walking to it. I don't know what her deal is, but she wanted a date and she got it."

"Well, if he does start going out with her, you can borrow some of the KT nicknames for her."

"From her days dating Cappie?"

"Yes."

"And they are? In case I need them."

Heath squirmed. "Mixed company. I *am* representing KT."

"So it's your responsibility to do something embarrassing."

"Well, if *you* won't…" And that got Heath to lean in and give a string of euphemisms not meant for mixed company, or for anyone with sensitive ears. Just in case Calvin needed them.

Just in case.

After so much buildup, the ceremony was remarkably short. Ted Griffin came up to the podium and gave a rather snarky speech about academic excellence, and trophies were passed out, allowing everyone to return to eating and chatting with the guests. Most of the engineers winning awards carried their plastic trophies around proudly, as if they hadn't cost the university $2.99, plus an extra dollar for the engraving, on a special bulk price Rusty negotiated. Dale beamed when he received his, oblivious to what the item actually was, or even that they spelled his name wrong. Casey decided not to point it out when he returned to his seat and instead just congratulated him.

Rusty finally located his lab partner after the speeches. "Do you still have your invite on you? Jordan wants to come."

"Why?"

He shrugged. "The formal sucks."

"Oh, right, the All-Greek Formal is tonight." Not like Feliks would be invited. "Tell her to call me when she gets here."

"Thanks, Feliks."

"My good deed for the night," Feliks said, and disappeared.

Rusty texted Jordan the information and Feliks's number, and finally took a seat at his table. The pressure of the event was officially wearing off, and the elation of meeting up with Jordan was rising. And he was hungry.

Casey appeared, taking the empty seat next to him. "What's up with Cappie?"

Biting into his baby carrot with an audible crunch, Rusty looked around, finally locating Cappie at some table of alumni, engrossed in a conversation with an old professor type, whom he didn't recognize off the top of his head. "Um, he's talking to people? He's a social guy?"

"Is he stalking me?"

"If he is, he's doing a really bad job, what with him not following you around and bothering you every minute or anything."

"He has no other reason to be here."

"Maybe he has obscure, Cappie reasons to be here. *I don't know.* I don't have, like, a psychic connection into his head. Also, open bar. And something about avoiding Rebecca."

"She went to the dance with Evan."

He finished another mini carrot. "Sucks for both of them." His feelings toward Evan, who had cheated on Casey with Rebecca, were well-known. At the moment, he really didn't care about either of them. "Is Rebecca still upset about her mysterious past with Rob?"

"I don't think we stayed long enough for it to come out in some drunken confession."

"Whatever. I mean, stay on your guard, but I think he's cool, in my limited experience. He was cool enough to escort you to another date, and that made Dale's night, even if he doesn't know about it."

Casey nodded. "He was."

"Casey, you're way better at dating and figuring guys out than I am. Why are you even asking me?"

"I don't know." She looked sad, or at least a little down. "I can't figure Cappie out. I never know what he's thinking. Why he's hanging around me, but insisting he's not."

"So ask him."

"He never gives me the real reason."

"Maybe he doesn't know it," Rusty suggested. "Sometimes guys have trouble expressing their feelings. Instead they do stupid things like punching other guys or waiting too long and letting a pledge go after the girl they're totally into and then having it blow up in their face and having their pledge depledge because of something they should have taken care of in the first place. And why is this surprising, anyway? Wasn't your original problem with Cappie that he was a spaz and took the relationship for granted? You dated Mr. Jerk Chambers because he seemed like he didn't. Because he was the opposite of Cappie."

Casey raised her finger at him. "No Evan spite. He doesn't deserve it—not anymore, anyway. And Evan is not the polar opposite of Cappie, and that was not the reason I went out with him. I loved him." She frowned. "That's not what I wanted to get into. But, yes, Cappie. Bad at commitments. No plans."

"Is it true Evan gave up his trust fund? Because normally I don't doubt my sources," he said, meaning Calvin but not naming him, "but that's crazy talk."

"I haven't asked him about it, but that's the story."

"So Evan makes commitments and can't keep them. Cappie doesn't make them in the first place." He shrugged. "I don't know what to say, except that these carrots are amazing. They're in some awesome sauce."

Casey picked up an unused spoon and tasted it. "It's cayenne pepper."

"Why does that name sound familiar?"

"You're allergic to it."

Rusty slowed his chewing. "I thought I was just getting a cold." A cold that made him light-headed. "Um, could you do me a big favor and get Dale? I think he has an EpiPen."

"Yeah," Casey said, dropping her purse in his lap. "I'm gonna get on that."

Cappie interrupted the older man he was talking to. "This has been really interesting, but I think I recognize that little guy they're loading into the ambulance. Do you mind if I excuse myself?"

"By all means."

There was some commotion, but Cappie was a master of getting around crowds, a skill honed from years of living in a small fraternity house that hosted large parties. In no time he was past the rubberneckers and at the ambulance, where an EMT put his hand up. "No other passengers."

"I'm his brother."

The EMT resisted for a moment, then let him in. The ambulance was parked, and it didn't look to be going anywhere. Rusty was on the stretcher, his face red and swollen. On one side was Casey, and on the other, Dale. Casey glared at him. "You are *not* family."

"Fortunately for us I'm not a Cartwright, but I *am* his brother."

"I'm fine," Rusty said. "I need to sit up."

"You're not fine, you're in shock and you've been shot full of epinephrine," Casey said. "You need to rest."

"Do I look bad?"

"Rest. Sleep. *Sleeeeeeeeep.*"

"You're not a hypnotist."

Dale looked up at Cappie. "He's a little…loopy from the shot. And obsessed with Jordan showing up."

"Dude, she's not expecting romance from a guy in an ambulance," Cappie said. "Are they taking him to the hospital? And also, what happened?"

"They said he should be fine." But Casey still wore a look of sisterly concern. "And, to answer your second question, bad carrots."

"I thought they were good," Dale said.

"That was the problem," Rusty said, his voice muffled by the swelling in his mouth. "They were awesome."

"He's allergic to one of the ingredients. Cayenne pepper. Only he didn't know they were spiced with it, so—"

"So that is totally something the pledges will have to memorize about you, Spitter. Obscure allergies. Very difficult." He put a hand on his arm, but Rusty didn't seem too observant of his surroundings. "Excellent work. Except for the whole actually eating stuff you're allergic to. That I can't recommend." He looked across at Dale, who was of course still holding his trophy as though it was an Oscar or possibly glued to his hand. "Maybe he's allergic to tacky trophies for track."

"Hey! It's supposed to be a dreamer. Reaching for the sky. The dean said it in his speech."

"Track trophies were all they had," Rusty said, and coughed

into his oxygen mask, "that didn't have some kind of sports paraphernalia. It was that or call a soccer ball a bucky ball." He giggled, which turned into another cough. "Bucky."

Cappie backed him up. "It is fun to say."

The EMT stepped in. "Does anyone know someone who can take Mr. Cartwright home?"

"He's not being admitted?"

"He needs a little more oxygen and then a lot of rest."

"I'll take him," Dale said.

"No!" Rusty really did try to stand up this time, and four sets of hands held him down. "I have a girlfriend. Gimme another shot of adrenaline. Then I'll, like, fly to her. Or leap. Like in the *Hulk.* The first movie. The bad one."

"Epinephrine is not for recreational use," Cappie said. "I may know some...people who've tried it."

"I'll take him," Dale repeated.

Casey reached into her pocketbook and produced some cash. "For a cab." She looked at her brother. "Are you going to be okay?"

"I have to see Jordan...Trans-Jordan. Egypt. Either one."

"Yeah, you definitely need to rest. Dale?"

"I'm on it."

At the EMT's insistence, Casey and Cappie left the ambulance, where Rusty would continue to rest until the swelling was down enough that he could be released—albeit into Dale's care, or the university's medical offices.

"The situation is being handled," Dean Bowman was calling, urging partygoers to return to the hall. "The student will be fine. Please return to the building."

At which point, Cappie broke out laughing, and Dean Bowman glared at him. "What?"

"I'm gonna save it," Cappie said, "and you have Rusty Cartwright to thank for that because my overwhelming concern for him is overriding my incredible desire to share some of the alumni's stories with you. For verification purposes." He didn't wait for Bowman's reply and went inside, Casey following him out of curiosity.

Cappie returned to his seat at the mostly empty table, where a professorial man with little hair on his head and a gray beard was making a fort of his mashed potatoes. "Casey Cartwright, meet Aristotle Izmaylov."

She didn't recognize the name, but she shook the hand of this apparently eminent man. "Hello, Professor."

"Oh, I'm not a professor anymore. Just a wealthy donor," he said, squinting through his thick glasses. "Hence the invitations I keep getting. And I wasn't even in engineering. I taught philosophy. To Dean Bowman and Ted Griffin, for better or worse. Your friend Cappie here is very interested in university history. Specifically the more embarrassing aspects. Not that I blame him. The rest of it is rather boring." He smiled at her. "So you're an engineer?"

"Political science."

"I was going to say there are not enough women in engineering, but now that really isn't my business, is it? There are plenty of women's studies professors to get angry about that. Political science is an excellent major. Not that far from philosophy, not too taxing. Enjoy your youth."

"Well, I am a senior," she said, a bit nervously.

"So cramming in the last excitement and planning for the future at the same time? A bit of a dichotomy, but nothing you can't manage, I imagine. I'm sure they've flooded this event with successful people to encourage you. Or perhaps it would be to their advantage to do the opposite, and charge you for a fifth year. Something Dean Bowman almost had to take."

"This is a great story," Cappie assured her.

"Not a particularly long one. The university briefly experimented with a system where students could invent their own majors—with a certain amount of planning and then presentation of the idea to a board, of course. This was before they had gender studies, so a number of people were trying that, as I recall. Your Dean Bowman tried for and made a comprehensive case for majoring in fun."

"Fun?" Casey parroted in disbelief.

"Yes. Fun. Had a rather long dissertation on it. He must have expected us to buy it, because he got halfway into senior year before bothering to present it to the board, where it was promptly rejected, despite my dissenting vote. So he had to cobble together another major by taking four philosophy courses in his final semester, which, in addition to the ones he'd already taken, allowed him to graduate on time. This was before fifth years were so trendy. If I were a betting man, I might have lost a good deal of money on betting on his success in the workplace. He's carved quite a niche for himself as an authority figure. And as he spent his days in my class with a beer-soaked brain, he might not remember me well enough to realize how amusing I find it."

"What do you do now?" Casey didn't know if it was appropriate to ask if he was retired.

"This and that," he said rather evasively. "I read. I write angry response articles to what I read. I make fake IDs." Without batting an eye he said, "Technology is really quite incredible. The definition of self can entirely be redefined through a concentrated effort on Photoshop."

“Please don’t encourage anyone present,” Casey said.

He shrugged. “Far be it from me to stand between man and his true nature. Which, at age eighteen to twenty, is to heavily consume alcohol. It’s never been any different and it never will be. Banning it just makes it more enticing, and I hate to see the promising young men and women of tomorrow in jail.”

“You were in a fraternity, weren’t you?”

“I predate the fraternity as you know it by some years, young Cappie. And in response to a good friend’s query, I would say only, drink up and be healthy, but all things in moderation.” He reached into his jacket and removed two cards, and they thanked him, and not until they were halfway across the floor did Casey bother to look at her card.

“He’s an advisor to the *Speaker of the House?*”

“Is that who that name is beneath his?” Cappie feigned ignorance. “I knew you’d want to meet him. People surprise you.”

“Sometimes they do,” Casey said, smiling just briefly before leaving him to check on her brother.

chapter eleven

Rusty felt as if he was floating—not quite out of his body, but certainly slightly removed from it.

"You sure you want to wait? Because we can go. I'm done. I have my…runner." Dale held up his trophy. "And the cards of some awesome guys. Maybe I'll see them next year. Do they invite the same people each year?"

"I don't know." And he couldn't really concentrate on anything except staying upright on the bench outside the entrance to the hall.

"Is that a guestlist-related 'I don't know' or a we-shouldn't-go-home 'I don't know'? Because you are still woozy there."

"Totally." But he didn't answer either question. It seemed like too much effort. He could imagine being home and he could imagine being back at the party, and either one worked, because it didn't require him to move. He could wait here, forever, for Jordan, and she would find him a thousand years from now, molded into the seat, his body as fossilized as the wooden beams of the bench he sat on. Fossilized trees were pretty and awesome to touch. He remembered a trip to Colorado, where, in a museum, he'd gotten to touch a trunk that had turned to stone. He must have been seven or eight, Casey ten or eleven, and she had pigtails and complained the whole way that he was hogging the Game Boy.

"I'm not hogging it." Looking up—itself almost an Olympic struggle—he saw Jordan's questioning face. "The Game Boy."

"He's not drunk," Dale said. "He's had a lot of epinephrine."

"I can be a tree," Rusty said. "I will be a tree. I just have to sit here long enough. Then, tree. I will totally be one. They'll put me in a museum of rock trees."

Jordan sat down next to him and took his hand, her skin incredibly soft. Maybe he thought that because he was turning into a fossil, and fossils were hard. "You need to go home," she said.

"You're beautiful." She was in a formal gown, with her hair up in some stylish bun with all the right pins, and she even had a smidgen of makeup on, even though he thought she looked fine without it. She just sparkled more. Normally she sparkled when she was smiling, but now she sparkled more, even when she didn't smile. "You sparkle."

"It's glitter." She tugged on his arm, as useless as that gesture would be. He was fairly sure his arm weighed a thousand tons, precisely, at this exact moment. "You need to go home."

"That's not very romantic," he said. "I wanted to be romantic. I *want* to be romantic."

"We can totally be romantic at your place."

"No atmosphere. Music's not as good." He added, "After-party."

"No after-party, Rus. Home. You have to go to bed and sleep for a very long time."

"No sleep. Clowns will eat me. I had a shirt that said that once. It was black."

"I'm sure it was. Come on."

"One dance."

"*Maybe*. Back at your place, I will consider that."

Rusty took that for a yes. Everything was possible, even him being able to stand, or precisely, be held up by his girlfriend and roommate long enough for him to be loaded into a cab. If they could lift a thousand tons, anything was possible. With that realization, he was satisfied.

Even after checking on her brother and leaving him on the bench with Dale, Casey wasn't fully satisfied until Dale returned to the hall, still clutching his trophy, and offered up an explanation. "Jordan showed. Thanks for the cab money. She's taking him back to the apartment." He shrugged sheepishly. "I couldn't convince him. He wanted to wait for Jordan."

"He is dedicated," she admitted. Rusty was dedicated to whatever or whomever he cared about, be it polymers or his current girlfriend. "Thank you for seeing him off."

"What else was I supposed to do?" He asked it as if it was his duty and did not require asking. "Thank you for coming. I know...well, Rusty kind of talked you into it."

She smiled. "I had a great time." Aside from nearly having a heart attack thinking that Max had somehow come to the awards, her turbulent feelings for Cappie and seeing her brother nearly hospitalized over the carrot dish, she actually had.

"Do you want to come to the after-party? I have to leave—set up with the band. It's not the Greek formal but—" he shrugged "—the music's okay. We've really been working on our sound."

"I'll try to swing by," she said, possibly meaning it. She could use a drink, but first she needed to get out of her heels. Unwilling to go so far as to kiss him, she hugged Dale.

"I really appreciated it," he said. "You must be really busy with your sorority and stuff."

"They'll deal."

"It's important—I mean, to be with people who really care about you," he said, and blushed before he left.

The party was wrapping up. The last-minute chatterers were swarming the more interesting alumni, others having been regulated to the status of "not donating" or "not offering me a job when I graduate" and therefore abandoned. Nothing kept her there, but she didn't immediately leave, instead looking around the room a final time.

At which point, she heard a crash and assumed Cappie had something to do with it. It wasn't quite glass shattering, but it was oddly similar. It didn't come from the room, but using her incredible investigative skills of following the remaining people who were also interested and better at finding things than she was, Casey ended up on the lawn where the cocktail hour had been held, sectioned off for events by trimmed hedges. The tables were still standing, but empty, and some of them had their tablecloths removed. In the center, the gigantic, half-melted ice sculpture was no longer on its perch. It lay in chunks on the ground, chunks that were quickly being snatched up by none other than Dean Bowman and the night's speaker, Ted Griffin, who held them in their jackets and took off in the other direction.

"Come on, you have to see this," Cappie said, appearing at her side—how did he always do that?—and grabbing her arm. To Casey's surprise, she didn't resist, and followed him to a nearby empty assembly hall, which had a wooden floor. Somehow, hockey sticks had been obtained, and what unfolded was a drunken, somewhat confusing game of hitting the chunks of ice back and forth between the players—Griffin and, of all people, Bowman. Professor Girard, the young anthropology professor, made a third.

"What is this?"

"Ice hockey," Cappie said. "A sacred and time-honored tradition that until tonight had been lost. Alas, it has been found."

Casey rolled her eyes. "What did you do?"

"Me?" Cappie was all innocence, or would be to the uninformed observer. "No way. It was all this guy." He gestured to Aristotle Izmaylov, the former philosophy professor, who was walking with a cane. "Hey, Professor."

"Hey, yourself, Mr. Cappie," Izmaylov responded. "And of what do I stand accused?"

"Spiking Bowman's coffee."

"That was Girard," Izmaylov said, gesturing to the professor who was busy trying not to get smashed into the wall by the other players, none of whom were wearing protective gear, and all in formal dress. "As to the discussion of traditional Cyprus-Rhodes ice hockey, I do believe the esteemed Mr. Griffin mentioned it first. Unfortunately in the presence of a person such as yourself."

"Bowman and Griffin used to steal ice sculptures from university events," Cappie said. "Then they would get together with a bunch of other guys and play until the ice melted. Nobody could remember the scoring system, if there was one. Another requirement was that you had to be drunk. So Dean Bowman walks by, and I ask him, and in front of Professor Izmaylov—"

"*Former* Professor Izmaylov—"

"—*former* Professor Izmaylov, he completely denies this, mentions something about juvenile delinquents and walks away. Griffin hears all this and starts cracking up, calling Bowman all kinds of names, and decides he has to do something about this."

"We decided we needed a man on the inside, not being university people ourselves," Izmaylov said, "so Cappie here was enterprising enough to approach Girard about it. He was immediately on board. Something about what Bowman said to him a few semesters ago in an academic review. He mumbled most of it so that it couldn't be held against him at a future date. Very intelligent man."

Casey squirmed as she heard a chunk go *crack* against the wall. "Is this legal?"

"Absolutely not. Bowman and Griffin were penalized some then-incomprehensible sum for damages, but spread over all their cohorts, it wasn't so bad. I wonder what it will cost now." Izmaylov grinned. "That wall's definitely going to need repainting. You know, Mr. Cappie, if you were to participate, it would be quite difficult for your dean to hold you responsible without implicating himself. With photography and all that." He held up his cell phone and took a picture of them. "Quickly, before he sobers up."

Cappie didn't need any other nudging, and grabbed a stick from the small pile and joined the game, which mostly seemed to involve who could knock the most ice against a certain spot on the wall that was growing ever darker and wetter. Dean Bowman didn't object to his presence, or really seem to notice.

"I should discourage him," Casey said, "but I can't come up with a good reason."

"And I don't like to be discouraging," Izmaylov said. "So we have a conundrum. Or we could just let youth be youth...and middle-aged academia be middle-aged academia." He grimaced as Bowman took a shot to the head, which looked as if it would hurt but didn't particularly slow him down, nor did he seem to notice. "I hope they're not under the false assumption that I'm keeping score."

"Is the lesson here that boys will be boys, no matter what their age?"

"Proverbial boys, yes, though I didn't have a lesson plan when I came here tonight," he said. "Though, I would also add perhaps that while one may remain an adolescent, it does not exclude a man from also growing up. Specifically when three people return to work on Monday—presuming no serious head trauma—and pretend nothing happened. We are all capable of the shift from maturity to immaturity, and the other way around."

"Should we stop them before the head trauma thing?"

"They'll run out of ice long before— Ow. That looked like it hurt. *Hopefully* they'll run out of ice long before we need to act."

True to former Professor Izmaylov's prediction, the ice did melt, and caused some slips and slides that ended the game with three out of four declaring themselves the winners and arguing about it. Cappie instead returned to Casey. "This is awesome."

"You have a black eye." Or what would soon be one, from the redness and the shot she'd seen him take.

"Yeah—from Dean Bowman. Best blackmail ever."

"Does it hurt? Can you see me? How many fingers am I holding up?"

"Two." He waved to the aged professor. "Thanks a ton!"

"Yes, and be well. And I do emphasize that last part."

"I would put an ice pack on it if I could find some ice," Cappie said. "Do you know where I can get some ice?"

He must have been tired, or a little confused, because he leaned on her excessively as Casey guided him out of the building and back toward the main road. "Are you sure you're okay?"

"I'm fine. Best black eye *ever,*" he insisted. "So what's up with you, Case? Missing the formal to come to what was apparently the best engineering party ever?"

"What's up with me? What's up with you and your sudden interest in alumni relations?"

"I think that panned out," Cappie said. "I'm thinking of switching majors."

"Engineering requires four years of study."

"That or something science-y. You know they're building Web filters to find and block pornography on the Internet? Who decides what's pornography? Obviously you would need to be some kind of expert on the digital experience."

"And you would be that expert."

"Precisely. There are whole fields open to guys with little technical experience but a willingness to learn, provided that learning involves female anatomy. Which my current major of women's studies will really help me with. Real résumé builder."

Casey was amazed. "Wow, Dean Bowman must have hit you pretty hard."

"I always talk about naked women. Or the prospect of seeing them. Ideally for money."

"Because you're talking about your résumé. That's sophisticated, near-graduate talk."

"Yeah, well, despite my best intentions the registrar informs me I will soon have enough credits to graduate. Unless I do something really spectacular in the failing department next semester—and believe me, I have not ruled it out—they might be hauling my ass out of here in June. Or maybe I could go out with someone at the registrar's office, then break up horribly—I'm good at horrible, traumatic breakups—and that girl who's there on Thursdays, I think she's a temp—"

"Cappie, stop."

"What?" He was walking on his own now, though following her lead. "You're the one asking questions. What are you doing here? Why are you talking to alumni? Why do you have extracurricular interests all of a sudden? Though I think this would actually count as curricular interests."

But she really didn't have a good reason. "I'm not like you." That was the best she could come up with.

"Because you understand all that was, is, and ever shall be Cappie?" He paused. "Just say it. The stalking thing. You think I'm stalking you."

"No."

"You've already said it. Other people have said it. I've heard that word so much tonight I'm starting to think a thesaurus should be mandatory for incoming freshman—"

"It's not that."

"Really? Well, okay, maybe you're right. Maybe some of my interests were related, somehow, in some extremely remote fashion to you. And either seeing you hanging out with Dale or not seeing you with Bob or Todd or whatever his name is."

"Rob," Casey said. "His name is Rob. And I am free to take whomever I choose to the formal, as I am currently single because someone wasn't interested in second chances."

She was referring to her closet admission—literally, in the

KT closet—of still having feelings for him and Cappie not rejecting her but being unwilling to commit. "I didn't say I wasn't interested," Cappie said.

"Well, you did. Pretty much by saying what you said. So I've moved on. To someone else."

"Yeah, that's worked out in the past."

"This is not all about me!" she cried.

"You seem to think it is."

"No, I mean, this is about you. And me. And not us. Because we, for some reason we both cannot explain, are not a couple."

And there it was. That was the sum of it, and neither of them could say it. Or anything. Crickets were audible in the silence.

"I don't want to fight with you," Casey said. "Can we not do this?"

"Okay. Truce. But I'm adding the words *Rob* and *stalker* to the list of words that are banned per the conditions of said truce," he replied. "And...also a gesture of goodwill might be finding somewhere that has Tylenol. Or something stronger than Tylenol. Very soon."

That was it. She melted before a confused, hurting Cappie, even if he was still lucid enough to make a speech. "Truce."

chapter twelve

Casey and Cappie did their best to put their fight— not their first, and likely not their last—behind them and focus on their quest to find a decent painkiller. Fortunately the campus drugstore was still open, with minimal offerings of aspirin and no ice, but a cold soda can worked just fine when wrapped in Cappie's tie and pressed against his eye. To her surprise, he was not willing to return to KT, but intended to keep his promise to see his buddy Dale perform at the engineering after-party—where she was, coincidentally, also going.

"Isn't KT having that medical-themed party?"

"While women in tight nurses' uniforms might distract me from the throbbing in my skull, they can't truly be appreciated with one eye covered by a diet soda can," he said. "And I promised Dale."

"So did I."

"Good, you can be my guide…lady? Woman of great esteem?"

"You were going to say 'dog.'"

"But I stopped myself!" He cracked a smile. "I blame Dean Bowman."

"For the black eye and possible brain damage?"

"No, just in general, but also that."

She laughed and helped him find his way to the party. It was a little surreal, to go from fighting to pain to laughter so quickly, but it was what made Cappie Cappie, and it was what made her love him. Just, not right now. Maybe.

Rob. She had to focus on Rob. Just not mention him in front of Cappie, as per their agreement. But she had to think about him, a lot, even though he was probably back in his dorm or whatever and she was going to the engineering after-party.

Which, it turned out, was quite a party. Far more typical of college life, it was filled with drunken students, some pretty buzzed from last call at the actual ceremony and the others trying to catch up. Darwin Lied, despite the name of the band, was well received. The science-minded students were either too drunk to care or probably thought it was meant to be ironic.

"I forgot—engineers are like overenthusiastic pledges who've never seen a girl before when they have an ounce of alcohol in them," Cappie said, taking a seat as soon as he found one. He removed the soda can, which was now warm, to reveal a thoroughly blackened eye. At least he was using his eye again, and it wasn't swollen shut. "They completely trashed the house—even by KT's illustrious standards—when we rented it to them. Destroyed Vesuvius and a lot of furniture. The former loss was worse. People cried."

"Egyptian Joe?" Egyptian Joe had created Vesuvius as his freshman project for KT, nearly a decade ago.

"He cried over the phone," Cappie replied, shouting a bit to be heard over the music. "Couldn't make the funeral."

"He still doesn't have a driver's license?"

"He has a driver's license. He just doesn't know how to drive."

"I think that's what I meant. You know, licenses can be used for something other than an over-twenty-one ID."

"Right. My powers of reasoning are…somewhat reduced." But that didn't stop him from grabbing a beer from the passing tray.

"Are you really okay?"

"I am really okay." He was lying, but that was okay. She wasn't going to get into an argument to talk Cappie into going home, having done that only an hour ago with her brother. Not yet, anyway. "Are you okay? I like repeating things. Possibly a sign of head trauma."

"I'm fine." She also accepted a beer. She needed a drink—desperately. She waved to Dale, who smiled but didn't stop playing. If anything, he played a little bit harder. Dale could be frustrating, but at least he wasn't complicated—unlike her current apparent charge, a wounded Cappie, looking adorably lost. "I think you should really consider the emergency room."

"No way," he responded. "If they have beer there, they are totally going to overcharge for it."

She sighed. At least one person out of two was willing to do the right thing.

"Go to bed."

"No."

"You're sick."

"Carrots can't kill me."

"You're home. Nothing's stopping you."

"You're stopping me," Rusty said, stumbling to his feet to properly face Jordan instead of remaining on the futon. His face was not as swollen, and the redness was decreasing, but there were bags under his eyes from an exhausted body. "I wanted this night to be romantic."

"I went to the All-Greek Formal with a bunch of scheming, gossipy pledges. How romantic is that?"

He looked sad, like a puppy who'd been bad and knew it. "I'm sorry I couldn't go with you."

"Rusty, it's a formal. It's pretentious and the dresses cost way too much. Who cares? We have other nights to be together. Not everything has to go to your ultraromantic plans."

"You don't like my romantic plans?"

"Sure...but spontaneity is good, too." She put a hand on his shoulder, mostly to force him back down, not show affection, even though she was showing affection by taking care of him.

"Allergy attacks are pretty spontaneous."

"You don't have to go that far in that direction, either," she said. "Although, it did remind me of our early days, when we both had an allergic reaction to those flowers and ended up in the hospital... But you don't have to try so hard. I like you for who you are. Sweeping romantic gestures are...well, not necessary all the time. Like when we have other obligations and you've been shot up with three different people's EpiPens."

"How not shocking was it that everyone seemed to have one?" he said, and she laughed. "You should have seen it. It was like a horde. A horde of highly allergic people."

"I would prefer to see you not involved in any EpiPen-related horde. I would prefer to see you in bed."

"Is that an offer?"

"Okay, now you're not being romantic *enough*." But they both knew exactly what she meant. Rusty needed to lie down and sleep for a very long time. Unfortunately, he refused to. "What is it with you?"

He actually stood, on two feet, without any help. "I'm getting a second wind. Hold on."

"What now?"

"I have to make it up to you. Missing the formal." He turned on his MP3 player and the stereo set it was attached to.

"You are way more obsessed with me missing the formal than I am."

"It's not about the formal." He finally found what he was looking for, and the music came on. It was soft—and romantic. "It's that magic moment of the last slow dance with your girlfriend."

She sighed. He had such an enticing smile. "And after this, you'll rest?"

"The last dance does signal the end of the night. That's why it's special."

"So, yes."

He grinned and took her hand, and they danced the remaining night away in the living room. There was no dance floor, or drunken antics of bored people behind them, or other couples around them. But there was music, there was dancing, and they had each other. For the last dance, it was more than enough.

Casey Cartwright remembered three previous dances, dances that hadn't ended halfway into the cocktail hour.

Freshman year she'd taken Cappie to a mixer. They were both pledges, and Evan and Cappie were nominally still friends.

That relationship would slowly disintegrate—mainly over her—but Casey didn't know that yet. She didn't know what the future held for her, only that it was college, and if she made it through rushing, it was going to be awesome. She had an adorable boyfriend and a bid at the coolest sorority on campus. Any freshman jitters were behind her, at least finals. She had even avoided the freshman fifteen despite all the late-night pledge snack-related study breaks. Cappie had told her he had never seen her look more beautiful, and she believed him.

Sophomore year, she'd moved beyond her freshman mistakes—taking the wrong classes, making the wrong friends and dating the wrong guy. Seeing Cappie still hurt, just a little, but it was easily forgotten when she was beside Evan, whose presence was near constant. Now that she was no longer a pledge, her responsibilities at ZBZ were exactly where she wanted them, and she had a guy in a more suitably matching fraternity than Kappa Tau. Zeta Beta Zeta and Omega Chi were the prom king and queen of campus, to use such adolescent, high-school terms, and Evan made her feel like a queen all on her own.

Casey remembered the dancing at a mixer junior year. It was tense, Evan's arms twitching slightly when he held her, almost too tightly, because he didn't want to lose her. And he was close. The only reason she was still with him after he slept with Rebecca was because Frannie had talked her into it, or so she told herself. In his worst moments Evan would remind Casey that she'd had her revenge by sleeping with Cappie again, essentially making them even. She'd never felt they were even. Evan had cheated on her, even if it was with only one person. He claimed to have had no feelings for Rebecca, but the sex had obviously thrilled him, or so it looked on the grainy video

Jen K. had sent to Casey's cell phone. Casey and Cappie just…fell in together, almost as if they needed to jog their memories of a better moment from their freshman year. Evan was right and wrong; it evened the score, but it didn't fix the problem. Soon after the formal, their relationship was over, and her future seemingly down the drain. Her life was no longer planned to be alongside Evan's in every way, from studying law together to marrying him. But at the formal itself, when they danced, the problems had gone away, if only for the length of the five-minute song.

And then there was Max, and last year's ZBZ formal, which might have made up for the disaster with Evan. At the time, it felt as though it did. She was in love with Max. She was convinced of it, but as it turned out, he was far more convinced of it than she was, to obsessive levels she couldn't handle. Or could she have tried harder? He'd treated her so well, but he hadn't made her smile like Cappie always did. He was reasonable in his expectations—he was a graduate student and she was a senior. It made sense to be looking forward, which was why he'd lavaliered her, even if it wasn't his tradition as an engineering grad, only to have her hand it back to him, as she'd handed one back to Evan not long before. The item that was supposed to be endowed with so much meaning now held little for her, except when it came to having her heart broken, often by her own doing. In other words, she was a walking romantic disaster. That wasn't Max's fault, and he hadn't deserved it. That was why she'd let him go.

"Why the long face?"

Here she was, her senior year, having abandoned the All-Greek Formal and the possibility of romance for reasons she didn't fully understand. Was it her promise to Dale? The fact that Rob had brought it up? The prospect of financial considerations? Sympathy for her brother, lost without his Jordan for a single evening? And she hadn't fled at the sight of Cappie, either. She wasn't afraid of him. She could handle him. She could be around him on the night of the formal and not immediately think of freshman year.

It occurred to her that she had to answer him. "Oh, just thinking about…memories. You know, formals. From the past three and a half years."

Cappie nodded. "I hear you." He paused, then added, "Actually I can't—this music is really loud."

"Head trauma."

"Yeah, I'm hearing that a lot tonight," he said. "But I think they're playing a slow song next."

"They have slow songs?"

"It was on his CD. Something about Jesus."

"Jesus likes slow songs?"

They were shouting to hear each other. "No, it's called something else. Definitely slow, though. Like a love song but with 'Jesus' instead of 'baby.' Maybe he stole the lyrics."

"I can't imagine Dale *stealing* anything."

"Good point." And just like that, the music level went down as Darwin Lied transitioned into their next song.

"This song is dedicated to some good people who raised themselves above their sinning brethren to be with me tonight," Dale said, "saved by the Grace of God. And epinephrine."

No doubt that got far fewer cheers than Dale wanted, but he was probably used to the college crowd by now.

"Still a decent band. A little weird, but decent." Cappie stood up and offered his hand. "Dance?"

"What?"

"I'm assuming you're familiar with the term," he said. "And you had to miss your special formal slow dance because of various people you are not dating, a bad selection for the main course and, let's face it, the opportunity to see a dean get a punch off on me."

"I think it was more like his elbow. In your face. Eye." But she did take his hand and follow him out to the dance floor. She was still in her formal dress, though her lipstick was long gone, and she was barefoot, and no attempt could be made to salvage her hairdo. Cappie was in a similar state of undress, his tie stuffed in his pocket and his shirt and jacket stained from being knocked around—she had seen him look better, but she had seen him worse.

And it was the last dance.

"What are you thinking about?"

"I'm having a little trouble imagining anything but the various implements that feel like they're being drilled into my eye. Why do you ask?" Before she could answer, he said, "What are you thinking about?"

She had to admit it. It was so hard to lie to Cappie. At least while they were slow dancing. "Freshman year."

"Wow. That is way beyond my cognitive abilities right now. Although, I am remembering attempting to pull off a bow tie."

"Yeah. It was purple."

"Did that make it worse or better?"

"It blended better, but I still don't recommend it."

"I remember…you saying that you liked it."

"I was neutral," she admitted, "but I wanted to say something nice. And I liked that you didn't look like everyone else. Tuxedos make guys kind of…clone-y."

"I thought it made us look like James Bond."

"You are way too shaggy to be James Bond. Which is fine. He's kind of a womanizer when you think about it. I wouldn't want to go out with him."

"But you'd sleep with him?"

She rolled her eyes. "He'd have to save me from something involving sharks or laser beams from space before I would commit."

"I can get goldfish. They die pretty quickly under my care, though. So I can get you dead goldfish, easy. Just give it a day. The laser rays may take more time. Do they *have* to be from space or can they be from a laser pointer?"

She giggled and leaned into him. Dead fish shouldn't have been so funny, she supposed, but it was late, she was tired and she was dancing her final dance of the night of the All-Greek Formal at an engineering after-party with Christian rock music crooning in the background. And just as she had at her first formal, she was doing it with Cappie.

"So, did you have a nice night?"

Evan escorted Rebecca from the formal, where things were wrapping up and people were moving to their various after-parties. Evan would probably just return to the Omega Chi house, but not before he took Rebecca back to ZBZ, because she was his date for some reason and it was the right thing to do. The thing guys who wore vests and ties on a regular basis despite a lack of dress code did. The thing knights did.

"Surprisingly so," was Rebecca's answer. "Thanks for the escort."

"From the way you framed it, I thought I was going to have to fight this guy."

"Yeah, and he left early. Maybe you're just very intimidating."

"I don't even know who this guy is. Which reminds me…"

She looked away, not eager to be reminded.

"You did promise."

"And you didn't get drunk enough to forget. I suppose some of that was my fault."

"Yeah, me keeping my cool and all is your fault." He shook his head. "You're Rebecca Logan. You're not afraid of your big sister or your president or Nationals or being drunk on YouTube—"

"I'm not a fan of dogs."

"Well, yeah." Their joint attempt to fight off a guard dog after Rebecca's car had been impounded with her much-needed laptop in it had been…memorable. Evan still wasn't sure how he'd gotten sucked in to helping her with that, but that had been the start of their new…well, he wouldn't exactly call it friendship, but friendly acquaintanceship. "The point is, you're not afraid of anybody. So why this guy, whose name now escapes me if I was even told it in the first place?"

"Robert. His name is Robert."

"And you promised."

"Not in writing!"

He stopped on the sidewalk, metaphorically and physically putting his feet on the ground. "What's up?"

"Would this stay just between you and me?"

Evan shrugged. "Who else would I tell?"

"Fine." And when she continued walking, he followed her. The campus was remarkably quiet for a Saturday night. "I was in high school, and Robert was a senatorial aid for the summer in my father's office."

He had a hunch where this was going, as nothing that included her father tended to be good, but he just said, "Okay."

"I had this friend, Lindsey. She was my idol. I was just a

lowly sophomore and she was a senior, but we'd been friends through my mom's family for years. She was accepted early to Yale, and it was her last summer, so my father offered her this ridiculously well-paying job pushing papers in his office because the only other thing to do in our hometown was be a camp counselor, and she needed money, so I talked him into it."

"Okay," he repeated, now even surer of the direction of this conversation.

"Robert and Lindsey started going out. At first I was jealous because he was kind of cute, but then just annoyed because it was my last summer to hang out with Lindsey and she was always hanging out with Robert. And this was all before I learned not to stop by my father's office late in the day and unannounced."

He didn't say anything. There was nothing he could say.

"I saw enough. Next to nothing is still enough. Lindsey was sleeping with my father's chief of staff, and Dad didn't want anyone to find out because there would be an ethics probe, so Robert was covering for both of them. He was never going out with her. He just said that to make her schedule seem busy and because my father threatened to fire him if he didn't—or so he said. Robert left for the summer, Lindsey went to Yale, the staffer took another job, and my dad…is still my dad. The one person I can't get away from."

"Did he apologize?" He added quickly, "I mean Robert."

"He did, but he acted like it was nothing, like I shouldn't be freaking out. Lindsey was eighteen and could make her own decisions. Like it was no big deal that my best friend—my aunt's goddaughter—was a slut."

"And how old was Robert?"

"Sixteen."

He had to venture into more dangerous territory to continue the conversation. "So what is he like now?"

"I don't know and I don't want to know."

"It has been five years. People change."

Rebecca glared at him, and she was so very good at that. It gave him chills even though he was expecting it. "Are you defending him?"

"No. You know I'm not. What he did was...well, he was a jerk. But that was four years ago and now...I don't know, maybe he's moved on. Matured."

"How do I know that?"

"You could ask."

"I have no obligation to him."

"Look, Rebecca," Evan said with a sigh, "you can do whatever you want. You can never speak to him again. But it sounds to me like he represents the problems you have with your dad, and that's what's really bothering you about him. You don't need anything left over from high school or your parents to ruin your life. Face him or forget him. Either way it'll be over with, and you can go to the next formal alone or with a date or however *you* want to do things." He added, "Though I did appreciate the invitation."

Rebecca rarely flinched, but after a moment, she did. "You're right."

"I am? I'm being told a lot lately that I'm not very motivational."

"Face him or forget him. It's a good motto." She gripped her purse extra tightly when she shook it for emphasis. "If it comes up—if he and Casey wind up dating—I will do something about it." She straightened up, not that she was slumping much. "Thank you."

"You're very welcome."

She let go of his hand, so he could go one way, and she the other. Charged with yet another secret to keep—college seemed to be full of them—he walked back to Omega Chi in time for the tail end of their after-party. It wasn't a particularly rocking event, but it was better than a quiet house.

"Should I ask how your date was?" Calvin said as Evan entered.

"I think by asking that you basically already did," Evan replied, removing his tie. "Yes, you can ask, and it was fine. Normal. Not bad or traumatic or devastating." Unlike his previous formal, when he was still dating Casey, which had been devastating because he was trying to avoid the oncoming disaster that would soon engulf them both and he knew it. "It was just a nice night." He shook his fist at his little brother. "No rumors about me and Rebecca. It was a favor. A fun favor, but a favor."

"You can get along with women and dance with them and talk privately with them without dating them," Calvin said as Evan passed him. "You just have to be related—or gay."

"I heard that," Evan grumbled, but decided not to confront Calvin, and instead turned in for bed.

chapter thirteen

Evan was long gone when Rebecca returned to the Zeta Beta Zeta house, as sororities and fraternities had to be situated with a mandatory length between them, an old-school rule still on the books. The house was lit but quiet, and she was alone—except for Robert Howell, sitting on the front steps.

"What the hell are you doing here?" Maybe it wasn't the most dignified opening shot, but at least it was a shot.

He stood, and he was much taller than she remembered. "Waiting for Casey."

"Didn't she invite you into the house?"

"No. She isn't back yet. That's why I'm on the porch." He moved aside so he wasn't blocking her entrance. "Look, if you want to pass me by, that's fine. I can deal. But can I ask why you're spreading rumors that I'm some kind of demon before I even get my foot in the door at CRU?"

"I did no such thing."

He huffed. "You said something to get everyone fired up, because that's all people have been saying behind my back. I couldn't get away from the formal fast enough."

"So that's why you let Casey ditch you."

"No. She wanted to leave and so did I, so we left. Hostile atmosphere, conflicting schedules—we each had our reason."

"Why should I believe you?"

"Because it's the truth?" Rob said. "Maybe we should start over. Hi, Rebecca, it's been six years—"

"Five."

"Five years. What have you been up to?"

"I'm not starting a friendly conversation with you."

"So there's only one kind of conversation you can have with me?" Rob put his hands on his hips. Yes, he was definitely taller than he'd been in high school. Her heels helped. "It's been five years! I haven't seen you. I've moved on with my life. Apparently you haven't."

"There's still my father."

He winced at that, but he recovered quickly. "Look, it was a long time ago. It's behind me now. If I could go back and…redo my decisions, I would try to make the right one. But I can't. And neither can you."

"What's that supposed to mean?"

"What's that supposed to mean? Who was more supportive of Lindsey, me or you? Who supported her rather dubious choices even after they were exposed?"

"She was eighteen years old!"

"Older than both of us! And we were her friends."

"I was her friend!"

"Then you were a terrible friend," he didn't hesitate to say.

"You abandoned her the moment she had a taint of scandal on her. Did you call her when she got to college? E-mail her? Or did you just cut her off?"

Rebecca stood, horrified, as she realized he was right. The little snot-nosed prick who had somehow developed into what everyone else imagined to be a mature, awesome guy was actually, somewhat, possibly a tiny bit right. Maybe. She hadn't called, or e-mailed, or anything. She'd felt betrayed by Rob, but she hadn't really cared about him. She'd cared about Lindsey, and Lindsey had betrayed her. Had not confided in her, had deliberately misled her. Everything that Lindsey was to her vanished the instant Rebecca saw her jumping off the chief of staff's lap when she walked into his office. Lindsey was dead to her—and Rebecca had treated her that way.

"I called a few times, and finally spoke to her once. She was trying to move on," he said. "She was pretty upset about you, though. So, yeah, I was a stupid kid, but you're hardly blameless." He moved in for the kill—though he did it in a rather soft voice. "I want to go on with my life—and I have, except you're in the same sorority as a girl that I happen to like and do not intend to do anything stupid with in any fashion. Are you going to stand in the way of that because of something that happened over summer vacation five years ago, or are you going to step aside and accept the fact that I've changed, and maybe even that I tried to do the right thing, but didn't know what the right thing was and didn't have anyone guiding me? And that it doesn't matter now, because it doesn't have anything to do with anyone but you and me? I'm just a normal transfer student, trying to make it up to the dean who arranged his transfer, keep his grades up and maybe meet a nice girl. Is that okay with you? Or at least acceptable?"

What could she do? Even if she told the story, she wouldn't come out well. No one would, and he would be forgiven when he went begging back to Casey, if he even bothered and didn't move on, leaving them all in his dust. Anything else she could say to slander his name would be a lie; the truth wasn't bad enough. He was forgivable, at least in someone else's eyes, maybe someone who hadn't had a father for a senator and a best friend as that staffer's temporary office slut.

"Fine," she said. "It's behind us. But I don't have to pretend that I like you."

"Fair enough."

"Are you going to go now?"

He said, "You know my story. I'm waiting for Casey. What's yours?"

Unable to answer him, she fled upstairs, away from Robert, her father and everything else she couldn't leave behind at Cyprus-Rhodes, no matter how hard she tried.

"Are you sure you can find your way home?" Casey asked, not for the first time.

Cappie, whose eye was not quite swollen shut, was walking uneasily, but he shored himself up to answer the question. "I'm fine. Well, no, I feel like someone's shoving a poker into my eye, but I can still see."

"Out of *both* eyes?"

"Yes, *both* eyes." If he wavered on the pavement as they walked, it was probably the last few beers for the road, and to take the edge off the pain. The bottle said not to mix the painkiller with alcohol, but that somehow made Cappie all the more eager to try it. "Besides, I can hear people shouting from a couple blocks away. And I'm supposed to walk you home."

"Because you're the chauvinistic male, and I'm the helpless female prey?"

"Wow. Add a dragon in there and we're in fantasy territory, Case."

She could only laugh at him. "You're the women's studies major."

"I want to change it, but it's just so tempting to stay in those classes. It's the professors. They try to drive me out and that just makes it more exciting."

"Or makes you more…failing."

"I have handed in every assignment and passed every test. If she fails me, she hates men and there's nothing I can do about it except sue her for gender discrimination."

"You're not serious."

He frowned, "No, definitely the aspirin-whiskey combo talking. I'll have to remember that one."

They paused at the corner before the street that led to the ZBZ house, Casey's home of three years. She could have walked home drunk and blindfolded—she even had once, as a pledge—and arrived safely, but that wasn't the point. Cappie was her escort, sort of, even if he wasn't her date. But they had danced, and she had no one else at the moment. "Thank you for walking me home. And for—whatever it was you did at the social."

"I did something?"

Cappie had acted politely, acceptably, and even with an air

of respect for his elders and peers. He had not shot her down but had boosted her, bolstered her conversations and recommended contacts for her. In other words, for some hours of the night, he had not been Cappie as she knew him. Or maybe that was what she expected of him after four years of college life, and nothing else—to play the fool even when he wasn't. But it would be rude, she realized, to imply that he usually acted like an idiot and he hadn't tonight and that was why she was thanking him, even though they both knew it. "Just—thanks. For whatever."

"Okay. I can accept a vague compliment. Not that it was a hardship. I mean, yes, missing a chance to get angry and punch someone at a formal is something I will just have to bear, but the chances of me seeing Dean Bowman drunk again are also pretty slim."

"You're not really planning to blackmail him?"

He shrugged. "I'll let him draw his own conclusions. And then blackmail him."

Despite herself, she laughed and held his arm, lost in a warm fuzziness she didn't dare examine until he said, "Wow, angry border guard."

At which point, Casey's night went considerably downhill.

Robert Howell, her *first* date of what seemed to be an evening succession of three of them, was standing on the porch steps, his hands in his pockets, looking rather apprehensive. Casey detached from Cappie, who was not too drunk to get the signal.

"Thanks for the walk," she said, far more formally than was in her heart.

"Safewalk. Thank you for helping KT fill its mandatory

community service hours." He waved to her and walked briskly off in the direction of his fraternity, another route she knew so well.

Casey spun around. "Rob!" She was legitimately surprised to see him, so that wasn't hard to muster. Her embarrassment was harder to stifle. "That was..."

"CRU doesn't have the Safewalk program."

"I know. He's...being dramatic," she said sheepishly. "That was Cappie."

"The KT president?"

Lying wasn't going to get her anywhere. "And, okay, my freshman-year boyfriend. He was at the engineering thing and Dale had to finish with his band so... What are you doing here?" She tried to put as much emphasis on the last sentence in as nice a way as possible.

"I was in the area," he said, and, in the darkness, it was hard to tell if he was angry, or ever had been, even though the lights for the porch were pretty bright. "And I wanted to say I was sorry."

"For what? *You* have nothing to be sorry about." She had plenty to be sorry about, or that was how she felt at this moment. "I know things were cut short but—"

"I didn't want you to think I was ditching you. It may have looked that way to your friends and people gossip and...you know..." He held out his hand, which she accepted, and stepped up onto the porch with him. With them both in full light, his better features—which seemed at the moment like all of them—were highlighted. He really didn't look mad. "I thought the other event was important to you."

"It was. And it was not supposed to be on the same night as the formal."

He nodded. "I heard. And...I may have had my own reasons for wanting to leave."

"Rebecca." It came out of her mouth before she could stop herself, but Rob was not disappointed. At least, in her.

"We go back," he said. "I should tell you the truth, so it's not some swirling rumor anymore. When I was working for her father, his chief of staff had an affair with one of her friends, and I covered for them. Rebecca found out, and nobody came out looking like a saint."

"Oh, wow, that's..."

"Not what you imagined?" He was so cute when he smiled, even if it was a painful smile. "I was young and I just did what the senator told me was good for my career. It was the wrong thing to do and I told Rebecca that five years ago and I told her again tonight. I can understand if she's having trouble putting it behind her. Senator Logan being her father and all."

"Uh, yeah."

"So...cut her some slack. And me, if that's possible."

"I wasn't holding anything I didn't know against you," Casey said. "Rebecca said it wasn't romantic from the start. She just wouldn't say what it was. And I was curious."

"I don't blame you."

"And I don't know what I would have done in that situation, either. So, okay, forgotten. Five years ago, not my business, whatever. I'll tell Rebecca—"

"Let her sort it out for herself. I think she needs to." And his eyes were oh-so-sensitive when he said it. It made him that much more adorable. "Anyway, I also wanted to thank you for the evening, the part of it we did share, and invite you to dinner next week. If you're not busy."

She jumped a little in her heart. "I would love to! And I am totally not promised to any guy on either night. I'm not promised to any guys on most nights—actually, all nights, right now, except you. I'm not normally—"

He stepped forward. "I understand. Next Friday, barring any disasters in university scheduling?"

"Yes, Friday night. Thank you. For everything." She was saying thanks a lot—just to different guys.

"Good night."

Her voice was very soft when she said it. "Good night."

Rob kissed the top of her hand—much like a knight—and left, to disappear in the direction of campus grounds and wherever he lived. His headquarters were unknown. He disappeared on the cool evening breeze of Cyprus-Rhodes, into the mystery from which he seemed to come. He wasn't mysterious—if anything, he more than adequately explained himself—but he wasn't *known*.

Like Cappie was.

Casey didn't have time to properly enter the house. Ashleigh pounced out of it like a tiger—an overexcited, overly friendly, but very aggressive tiger. "So? He waited for you for, like, ever. Isn't that adorable?"

"It is. And a little stalker-ish." She winced at her word. Definitely overused.

"Yeah, but there has to be, like, something a little *not* okay for him to be so awesome. Otherwise you would know it was fake. No guy is that great. So his flaw is what? Perseverance? He came back as the formal was ending—and I guess the boring engineering thing."

"It wasn't boring. I was pleasantly surprised. Things were—pleasantly surprising." And unpleasantly complicating. "It was…nice."

Nice didn't begin to sum it up, and smoothed over a lot of rough edges. The persistent signals that her future beyond CRU and ZBZ was coming, and she had to prepare for it. And the one to guide her through that, or to it, had been, of all people, Cappie. He was nice, the people she met were nice, and at the end of the evening, even Rob was nice. So why did she feel so uneasy?

The evening had been complicated. For the moment, that was all her weary body and mind could accept, but she knew she could not avoid the persistent questioning of Ashleigh. It was best to roll with it—or more specifically, to let Ashleigh do the talking. "So how was the formal?"

"It was so awesome! You should have stayed. Or, I guess, if you had a good time—but you would have been cute on the dance floor with Rob."

"I seriously think you have a crush on my almost boyfriend."

"Almost? Case, his hands might have not been all over you, but his eyes were. And not in a creepy way. A guy way, but, like, a cool guy way. A way I would be fine with. The way Fisher looks at me sometimes when—"

"Ew, Ash, stop right there."

"Right. Where was I? So, the old ZBZ pledges totally want to come back as soon as they can move out of the IKI house, and it turns out they pronounce it 'icky,' too, or have started since Frannie broke up with Evan so now he's not paying for anything the house needs. And Katherine from

Panhellenic was seriously pissed at their behavior, but didn't do anything about it.

"Rebecca came with Evan, you know that—what was up with *that?*—but he was totally like, 'I'm doing this favor.' They never really went out, did they? They just had sex. *Anyhoo,* there was pretty much that, and Cappie never showed and Heath was KT president instead for one night."

"Cappie was at the engineering event."

"Really? Why?"

"Why indeed?" Casey didn't put so much emphasis on it. She didn't want the question actually delved into. Ashleigh would speculate, and possibly be right.

"Is that why he walked you home? Wait, that thing must be over by now."

"After-party. Dale invited us."

"Wait," Ashleigh said, "you went to the formal with Rob, the engineering dinner with Dale, and the after-party with Cappie?"

Casey sighed. "It just sort of…happened."

"Case, a lot of things with you and Cappie *sort of happen*. I don't sort of happen into things with my ex-boyfriends."

"Ash, you have one ex-boyfriend. Can we just drop it?"

"Fine." Fortunately, Ashleigh didn't put up a fight and moved right along. "Did you know Calvin used to go out with Heath? Though I guess they didn't go out because they didn't actually, you know, go places because Calvin was still in the closet. This system is stupidly backward. Calvin couldn't dance with anyone. I mean, that he would want to dance with as a date dance, not a pity dance for a girl who can't get a date."

"That is sad."

Ashleigh went on for a little bit longer, but it sounded as if Casey hadn't missed much. And she'd had her own dance, albeit not with Rob but Cappie, and not at the formal, but a very informal party with a bunch of drunken engineers. Relieved of her duties of keeping up with all things social at ZBZ, Casey went to the bathroom to brush her teeth, only to find Rebecca there—similarly in pajamas, but glaring at her.

"What?" She threw up her hands. "What did I do now?"

"Are you going out with Rob?"

"We went out tonight and we are planning to go out again at some future point. Draw from that what conclusions you want." Casey looked down at her toiletries bag, trying to avoid the glare of doom. It had its own way of speaking for Rebecca. "What? He's a nice guy. And what happened with you in high school or whatever, he's past it, even if you're not."

"I didn't say that."

"So this interrogation about my date for the evening is just for fun?"

"It seems like you had a lot of dates for one evening."

"And you went with Evan. Whom I could still be pissed at if I even had the energy for it right now—which I don't. We both went out with guys the other person didn't like. We're even—if it's even a game, but I don't think it is. Yes, I'm going out with Rob. Deal."

"You're going to get burned," Rebecca said.

"And you're heading down a wonderful road with Evan Chambers, king of fidelity. Oh, no, wait, you're the one who made him lose that title."

"He was doing me a favor. Like you're going to say Cappie was doing when he walked *you* home."

"I…" But she didn't really have an answer to that. Not immediately anyway. "I appreciate an escort. And guess what? Rob was fine with it. Rob was fine, Cappie was fine and I'm fine. The only one upset by my evening is you."

Rebecca's retort was not immediate. She was shoring up her anger, then swallowing it, her voice pure determination. "It won't end well," was all she said in the end, and stormed off, leaving Casey alone.

"Intense. Not that she ever isn't."

Casey turned to Ashleigh, who appeared from around the corner, no doubt listening in on at least part of the conversation that had passed. "She's not right, is she?"

"You like two guys. One of them is going to be disappointed. It's math. And life. Life and math. You just have to decide who it's going to be," Ashleigh said, not nearly as worked up about it. "But I think we both know who has a hold on your heart."

Once there was quiet in the house, Casey went to bed, a peaceful end to a far less peaceful night. When she closed her eyes, she conjured up an image of Cappie but as she drifted off, she realized she had no idea what the dawn would bring, or what she would do about it.

When Cappie knocked, Dale answered. Usually, after noon, if Rusty wasn't at the house or at class, it was a fair shot that he would be the one to open the door to his apartment with Dale. Not the case now, at one in the afternoon on a Sunday.

"Shouldn't you be at church?"

"Online worship services," Dale said, sipping on a juice box. "The effect can be amazing if you have really good speakers. All the harmony of the choir but devotional privacy. Do you want to come in?"

"Sure." He was slower moving than he normally was this morning, mostly for anything head-related, and not just because of dead brain cells.

Dale puttered around the kitchen like an old woman. It was a slightly unfair comparison, but it was true. "Do you want some ice or something?"

"Thanks, but it's way beyond the point of ice." His black eye was pretty prominent on his face. Dale probably figured it was from the KT party. "I'm checking on Rusty. He was a little down-and-out last night."

"He woke in this panic, thinking he'd dreamed the whole night and now he had to go get ready and pick up the ice sculpture. Then he saw my trophy and went back to bed." Dale was possibly the only person at CRU who kept his refrigerator stocked with Juicy Juice packets, one of which he gave to Cappie. "He seemed okay. I gave him juice."

"You are the juice man," Cappie said, trying to push the tiny straw out of its tiny plastic casing.

"Is your eye okay?"

Cappie settled on the futon. He had wondered when Dale was going to mention it. "Yeah. You can't go into battle without a few bruises. And a little mysterious swelling. Is there a Bible quote about that?"

"'O virgin daughter of Zion, how can I comfort you? For your wound is as deep as the sea,'" Dale said. "Lamentations.

Second book, I think. I'm really behind on my memorization quizzes. All of these...otherworldly distractions."

"I was going to say to cure swelling, but, yeah, I see what you're saying. You could always move to a new apartment. You have a pretty good setup here, but I'm sure you could feng shui the hell out of a new place."

"When you bring heathen arts into your home, you push Christ out. Or that's what Grandma Kettlewell said when my mom bought her one of those bonsai trees at a street fair for her birthday. Maybe she just didn't like the gift." Dale settled in to the futon. "And I got to go with Casey, which was pretty awesome, even if there was that whole thing with Rusty. It wasn't his fault," he said, and leaned in. "This is not, you know, something I would normally ask you, but have you ever had a truly enchanting woman in your life, in, like, all the wrong ways?"

"Um, yeah. Story of my life, Dale."

"So what do you do? How do you fortify yourself against her persistent attacks? I don't think she knows she's making them, but she is."

Cappie was pretty sure Dale was delusional if he was thinking about Casey hitting on him. He blamed the sugar. "Uh, if she's making them then she knows she's making them. I don't think she was making them."

"That's right, she spent the entire night with you." But Dale didn't sound angry about it, just down. "I was fooling myself again, hitting on your girlfriend."

"She's not my girlfriend."

"What about when I do find the right woman? How will I know to act? I find someone like Casey, who's spoken for, and I can barely do anything. Imagine if I found someone I could actually pursue. What's she going to be impressed by? My trophy?" Dale said. "There's this girl in my Introduction to Algorithms class who's kind of cool. I mean, I get a feeling when I look at her, but I don't want to blow it. And I think she's sending me signals. I know in my heart that I have to be strong, but it's like there's this other force that's driving me to her. I would say it's evil, but I really don't want to hurt her feelings."

"Then put up or shut up," Cappie said. "Sorry to be harsh, but it's go time. I would be doing you a disservice by saying anything else. If she wants to be with you, you have to either be with her or reject her."

Dale wasn't thrilled with this answer, but he wasn't mad at Cappie, either. "I need to pray."

"Go on, yon faithful Christian soldier."

Dale disappeared up the steps, trusting Cappie to show himself out.

"Doing you a disservice? What kind of bullshit is that?"

Rusty emerged from his room. He looked paler than usual, but not red or swollen up like a football as Cappie had last seen him. "What?"

"Dale's trying to reconcile his wholesome Christian values with his sex drive. Okay, good advice, make a choice, but you are *so* the last one to give it."

"I was going to say, nice to see you, how are you feeling, little bro? But instead I'll just observe that an allergy attack can make you quite ornery, and forgive you for bitching me out for a minute there."

"It's good advice, but you should take it yourself first," Rusty said, not relenting. "Casey lives in this state of romantic agony because you won't commit, for reasons that have never satisfied her, and you don't have half the excuses Dale has."

"Spitter, are you seriously trying to hook me up with your sister again?"

"I'm just saying, put up or shut up," he said, taking Dale's seat. "And don't, like, be shocked when she doesn't want you around, being all ambiguous, or when she has a new guy in her life. Which I don't even want to think about, because she's my sister, but I have to because both of you throw it in my face without even mentioning it."

"Casey doesn't need me. She has some guy—Rob. Generic name, good suit, appropriate amount of concern for her needs."

"She's only going out with him because she doesn't want to be alone and you're the reason she's alone. And maybe it would be fine if you just dumped her and you both got on with your lives, but are you seriously going to tell me that you went to see Dale get an award because you wanted to support him? You can expand your horizons at plenty of pretentious university events that do not involve my sister, and we both know it, and Casey knows it and it drives her crazy."

Cappie knew better than to try to fight Rusty point-by-point when he was on a rant. "It doesn't matter. She's happy with another guy."

"She'd dump him in an instant if you would commit to anything beyond this crazy game you have now. So do us all a favor—put up or shut up. And, no, this is not the antiallergens talking."

"What do you want me to do?"

Rusty didn't have an answer. Or he wasn't willing to give

one. "Just don't break her heart—again." And rather dramatically, he left.

There was something particularly final to Rusty's comment, and Cappie knew it: there were only so many times a heart could be broken.

★★★★★

Stay tuned for more GREEK!
Look for
GREEK: BEST FRENEMIES
by Marsha Warner
on sale in August 2010.
Only from Harlequin Teen.

New York Times bestselling author

RACHEL VINCENT

SOMETHING IS WRONG
WITH KAYLEE CAVANAUGH

SHE DOESN'T SEE DEAD PEOPLE, BUT...

She senses when someone near her is about to die. And when that happens, a force beyond her control compels her to scream bloody murder. Literally.

Kaylee just wants to enjoy having caught the attention of the hottest guy in school. But a normal date is hard to come by when Nash seems to know more about her need to scream than she does. And when classmates start dropping dead for no apparent reason, only Kaylee knows who'll be next....

THE LAST THING YOU HEAR BEFORE YOU DIE

Look for Book 1 in the Soul Screamers series
Available now wherever books are sold!